Uncertain Outcome

Uncertain Outcome

Ulla Bolinder

Translated from the Swedish by

Eric Swanson

in collaboration with the author

Originally published in Sweden as *Oviss utgång*
by BoD 2021
© Ulla Bolinder 2021
English Translation © Eric Swanson 2023
Cover photo: Pixabay
Publisher: BoD – Books on Demand, Stockholm, Sweden
Print: BoD – Books on Demand, Norderstedt, Germany
ISBN: 978-91-7569-733-8

It is done. Nothing can undo it;
nothing can make it otherwise than as it was.
Charles Dickens: *David Copperfield*

FRIDA

I have received a letter. An ordinary letter, in an ordinary envelope with a stamp on it. Mats Wiklund, who has served a long prison sentence for the murder of his ex-partner, wants to meet me to discuss a book project. He has read my book on abuse of women and has got the idea that I am the right person for the task of writing about his case. I don't know why he wants a book to be written about it. If I agree to meet him he will explain, he writes.

The murder didn't receive much media attention. It was considered a so-called family tragedy that isn't regarded to have such a great public interest. At the time of the murder, Mats Wiklund and Sandra Brolin had separated and lived in different places. Their six-year-old daughter had stayed with her mother, and Wiklund, who is a licensed psychiatrist – or was, because he had his license revoked – had moved to a flat near the hospital where he worked. All this he writes in the letter to me, and I don't know more, except that he was convicted of the murder in spite of his denial.

Why did he choose me? Why do I get a strange feeling that I don't want to get involved with him? What causes that feeling? How he expresses himself in the letter? That I don't know what he is after?

When I googled, I didn't find much. No photo of either him or her and no details about the murder. I simply have to listen to what he has to say, if I want to know more. And I am a little curious, at the same time as I feel resistance and discomfort.

How much has he found out about me? What does he know? I am not a well-known, established author. I am not really a writer at all. The book on abuse of women is the only one I have written and published. It isn't enough to form an opinion about me.

And what is he after? Being released prematurely it can't be. He will soon have served his entire sentence. Is it perhaps to be granted a new trial and be cleansed and obtain redress and damages he hopes for? In that case, he needs a lawyer or a digging journalist. I don't understand his motives, and that irritates me.

He was convicted in spite of his denial, but that doesn't necessarily mean he is innocent. According to the maxim of Ockham's razor, you should, if faced with two possible explanations, choose the least complicated one. That choice is supported by the general theory of probability, which states that a hypothesis chain becomes more and more unlikely the more unknown factors are introduced into it. And the simplest explanation in Mats Wiklund's case is that he was the one who did it.

Would I be able to be open to a person who may have murdered? It's one thing to listen unreservedly to victims, like the women I interviewed for my book, and quite another to listen to perpetrators. When you know what it might look like after their ravages, it's difficult to feel anything but disgust and contempt. If it turns out that the murder of Sandra Brolin is the end of a long period of repeated beatings, I am not going to help Wiklund. Not if his appearance or behaviour arouses disgust in me either.

As for the question of guilt, I assume that he is guilty. I take for granted that there was strong evidence against him that caused him to be convicted. But the crucial thing is whether I get a positive or negative impression of him.

I haven't decided yet if I will meet him. He sent me his contact information, so the only thing I have to do is answer yes or no. I don't really understand why I hesitate.

I have talked to Wiklund on the phone. His voice was low and warm. Was it his professional voice he used, or is that how he sounds in private?

He wants us to meet. The possibility for inmates to receive visits and obtain leave from prisons and institutions has been limited during the pandemic, but now that the vaccination rate has increased, new conditions apply. After the first of June, leave on their own is granted for inmates who have been vaccinated with the first dose at least three weeks earlier, or after undergoing covid-19, diagnosed with a PCR test or with an antigen test. I didn't ask which category he belongs to because that's none of my business.

The leaves of absence that he receives are part of the transition and reintegration into society. It isn't a right, and those on leave must call the institution at certain times or report to, for example, a prison, a police station, or a probation office.

We have decided the day, time, and place. Because of the coronavirus, he suggested that we meet outdoors to reduce the risk of infection, but if he has been vaccinated or has had the disease, I am not worried.

At work, we have been instructed to use hand sanitizer and keep our distance and not stay too many people in the same room. No one uses a face mask. At all meetings we follow the instructions, but then everyone sits close together in the coffee room as usual and doesn't seem to have a thought about the risk of infection, so I don't understand how it should work. Not everyone has been vaccinated yet, and some may have to refrain from it for health reasons, so the danger is definitely not over.

FACEBOOK

Eva Andersson
Yeeezzz! Now I have finally got a vax appointment!

Karolin Östberg
Congratulations!

Linn Jörgensen
Wonderful!

Fred Adler
Welcome to the club!

Kerstin Sundgren
Great! I get the first shot on Monday. The Lord be praised!

Ove Jansson
I'm already fully vaxed. It feels safe.

Lennart Lindh
Took the second one yesterday and feel as strong as superman.

Astrid Nyström
Good for you, Eva, hope everyone takes their responsibility. Also got 2 shots. I also had covid in March last year with fever, cough, pressure over the chest, difficulty breathing, loss of taste and smell and extreme fatigue. Still having problems. So this is not a game.

Margareta Södergren
My heart warms every time someone uploads

a picture with the patch on the arm.

Måns Pettersson
Good, Eva! If we don't take our responsibility in solidarity, we will never get rid of this pandemic!

Mimmi Gustafsson
The shots feel like a godsend that everyone should receive with joy and gratitude.

Linda Palmqvist
The vaccines haven't been fully tested and the studies won't be completed until 2022, 2023.

Ylva Borén
How many of those who choose to take these injections know that they are part of the world's largest medical experiment on mankind? How many people know that there should be an informed consent to this with all information about side effects? How many people know that a natural immune system is important, which is better than what you get from this "vaccine"?

Fred Adler
Who are you listening to? Established scientists who have worked with vaccines for years or people who sit and google on the couch at home?

Berit Schedin
Yes, keep your opinions to yourself Ylva, and don't destroy something that society has built on science.

Tomas Bergman
A thing that can't be questioned isn't worth believing.

Linda Palmqvist
Note that it is the VACCINE we are questioning, we
who refrain, not those who choose to be vaccinated,
while the vaccinated attack US. That says a lot, I think!

Mimmi Gustafsson
Vaccine is the best we have invented for public
health. Nothing else is so good, says Anders Tegnell.

Ylva Borén
Johan Giesecke, who was Sweden's state epidemiologist
95–05, said in an interview in May 2020 that when it
comes to diseases, it's always better to have had the
disease than the vaccine. The infection provides a more
complete immunity than the vaccine.

Fred Adler
Block the trolls, Eva!

Måns Pettersson
Yes, but then when the vaccine came, he changed his
mind and started collaborating with the public health
authority.

Tomas Bergman
"I have my principles, but if they don't fit, I have
others." (Groucho Marx)

Fred Adler
Just take the damn vaccine so we can start living
normally again sometime!

FRIDA

We met in the park and sat down on one of the benches near the fountain with as far distance as possible between us. Neither of us wore a mask. The vaccination has been going on for quite a while now, but it hasn't been my turn yet. I need to find out more before I decide what to do. I know far too little about both the virus and the vaccines to be able to make a well-grounded decision.

But finding information isn't easy. Google doesn't work, I have realized, with the enormous amount of both factual and dubious information available online. I have found a discussion group that seems serious, and I continue to follow my friends on Facebook and read their posts when the question comes up. I hope that will be enough because I don't have time for more than that right now.

I don't know for sure, because I was never tested, but I think I had covid-19 last spring. I was home from work for five weeks, until I felt better and had no clear breathing problems anymore. I didn't have a fever, but I was extremely tired and had strange symptoms that I didn't recognize. The most unpleasant was the pressure over my chest and the smarting pain in my lungs, which came and went, and that I lost all strength. So, my starting point for a possible vaccination is that I may have become immune then and don't need to be vaccinated. But I don't know if this is how it works, or what alternative the experts recommend when you have already had the disease.

THE DIALOGUE

FRIDA: Is it okay if I record our conversation? If I decide to accept the assignment, it's good to have everything carefully documented from the beginning.

MATS: Yes, of course. First, I want to say that it isn't easy for me to ask for this. But I have had plenty of time to think, both about what happened and about my current situation, and I have come to the conclusion that I need to do this to help myself.

FRIDA: Okay.

MATS: I'm not saying you should trust me. You can take part in all the material and talk to whoever you want and form your own opinion. If you are willing to try, I'll give you access to all the documents you want.

FRIDA: Okay. But then I first want to ask you why you chose me. What do you know about me?

MATS: Not much more than that I have read your book.

FRIDA: And what did you think the book said about me?

MATS: Yes, what should I say… That you can listen, I think. If all these poor women wanted to tell you their story, it must be that way. And that you write well. Another reason is that you live here in town so that we can easily meet.

FRIDA: Okay.

MATS: Why did you choose to write about abuse of women? Have you been abused yourself?

FRIDA: No, I haven't. But I have a workmate who has experienced it, and that's how I became interested. She's one of the women in my book.

MATS: What do you do when you're not writing?

FRIDA: I work at the Social Insurance Agency as an administrator. Writing isn't my main occupation.

MATS: So that book you wrote in your spare time?

FRIDA: Yes, and so it must be with this one as well if it comes off. So you can expect it to take some time.

MATS: Yes, that's okay.

FRIDA: You were convicted in spite of your denial. Are you hoping for a new trial now?

MATS: No, I haven't thought that far.

FRIDA: Because you probably know... There are many murder convicts who claim their innocence, but the cases are difficult to take up for review without sufficient reason. In that case, it must be possible to point out serious and obvious deficiencies.

MATS: Yes, I understand that.

FRIDA: According to the so-called principle of steadfastness, a judgment that has gained legal force should in principle be impossible to tear up. But according to another principle, the principle of truth, it should be possible to correct erroneous judgments, and if it is to the advantage of the convicted person, the principle of truth should weigh more heavily.

MATS: Mm.

FRIDA: If there are important circumstances or new evidence that is so strong that it would probably have led to a different outcome if the evidence had been known when the case was decided, the court can grant a new trial so that the case is tried again.

MATS: Yes, I know.

FRIDA: But not many people have succeeded in doing so, and everyone who has got ahead with it has been helped by digging journalists. But I'm not a digging journalist.

MATS: No, I know that.

FRIDA: Why didn't you turn to a journalist instead? Or to a lawyer?

MATS: Because it isn't a new trial that I'm primarily out for.

FRIDA: Yes, sorry, I know you said that. What are you out for then?

MATS: To create an overall picture of all the circumstances so that everyone is free to draw their own conclusions.

FRIDA: Why?

MATS: For my daughter's sake. And for my own.

FRIDA: How are you thinking?

MATS: I want her to know the truth about Sandra and me. Not by me, but by what others have to say about us. I want her to know how we were, and that it wasn't me who killed her mum. Or that she can at least imagine the possibility that it wasn't me. She thought she saw me do it, and at that time, when she was little, I didn't want to question and rebuke her. In any case, her testimony wasn't decisive for the outcome. I didn't want her to start doubting herself. I told her it wasn't me who had done it, but I didn't try to convince her when I noticed that she didn't believe me. I don't know what she still remembers, or what others have said to her, but when I come out, I want her to have the opportunity to form her own, and perhaps new, opinion of me. And she can't do as I ask *you* to do now. She can't look up people who were present at the time and ask to hear their views on the matter. But she can read about it in a book, if and when she wants, only that book exists. Do you understand?

FRIDA: Yes.

MATS: Have you read the preliminary investigation?

FRIDA: No, not yet.

MATS: There you'll find the names of people you can contact. I can probably suggest others as well. But it isn't certain that everyone wants to be interviewed or remembers very well how it was like.

FRIDA: No. Do you want me to look up your daughter too?

MATS: Yes, if you want to and she agrees.

FRIDA: Have you had contact with her over the years?

MATS: No, not at all. I think she was first forbidden and then advised against meeting me.

FRIDA: By whom?

MATS: By her grandmother, who has taken care of her since Sandra and I disappeared.

FRIDA: What about your own parents then?

MATS: Both have lived in Spain for many years and don't know much about what happened.

FRIDA: Okay. Now I'll go home and think about what I want to do, and you'll be notified as soon as I have decided.

FRIDA

How did he look? How did he act? What feelings did he send out? What impression did he make on me?

He was dark-haired and quite tall. Had thin face and grey-blue eyes. Looked sympathetic. And his voice was like the first time I heard it, when we were talking on the phone.

A murderer can look sympathetic and have a warm and confidence-inspiring voice. A murderer can look good and have a friendly and accommodating manner. A murderer can very likely sound vulnerable and loving when talking about his children. There are very nice women abusers and very nice murderers. I know this from personal experience.

I was a little nervous and started quite uncalled-for rattling off a lot of facts about the judicial system. I regretted it afterwards. It's not a new trial he is out for. But now I know and understand his purpose.

I understand what he wants, but I don't know who he is. He has been convicted of murder, and you won't be that without cause. It happens that people are convicted on only circumstantial evidence when there is no conclusive technical proof, but how it was in his case I don't know yet.

In the Swedish judicial system, it's the so-called principle of objectivity that applies, which means that the prosecutor must take into account facts that speak both for and against the suspect's guilt before prosecution. During the trial itself, the principle of immediacy applies, which means that the only thing the members of the court have to decide on is what's presented during the main hearing. Since it is the prosecutor who chooses what's to be presented to the court, it's in principle only his or her conscience that decides what's to be included and what's to be omitted, and it's up to the defendant's defence councel, who has considerably less resources to make use of, to find flaws in the arguments and to discover circumstances that the prosecutor has chosen to withhold.

I don't know on what grounds Mats Wiklund was convicted. The examination of evidence in Swedish law is as good as free, that is that anything may be used as evidence, and the value of evidence isn't regulated by law. If there is no clear technical evidence against a person, but the court considers that the only possible explanation is that the defendant is guilty of the crime, he can be convicted anyway. I have to read the judgement to find out how they reasoned in Wiklund's case. He made a positive impression on me, so I guess I will agree to what he asks, now that my curiosity is aroused, and I would like to write a book again.

I have informed Wiklund that I agree to undertake the task. I have requested the preliminary investigation report and the judgement and received both. When I have read the interrogations with witnesses, experts and Wiklund himself, and studied the technical investigation, which hopefully gives a detailed description of the crime scene in words and pictures and of all the findings that were made, such as murder weapon, fingerprints, shoe prints, fibres, DNA, and other things. I will try to get hold of the responsible investigator and ask for a meeting. I hope he hasn't forgotten the case and can give me information about his personal impressions and thoughts about it all.

Hans Thorén

Here is some information. Last year, Sweden had a clear excess mortality according to the National Board of Health and Welfare's report on causes of death in 2020. A total of just over 98,000 people died, which can be compared with the average in 2015–2019, which was just over 91,000 deceased. So that the coronavirus has left its mark is quite clear.

Per Eriksson

If you count correctly, we definitely had no excess mortality in Sweden in 2020. Firstly, unusually few people died in 2019, which always means that more people will die the following year. Secondly, the population hasn't been taken into account, which you absolutely must do if you are to prove excess mortality. Thirdly, one should have gone back much further than to 2015. Then it had been seen that in the years 98–03 the mortality rate was 1.1 %, and 1993, which was a severe flu year, 1.12 %, while 2020 was "only" 0.95 %. All according to the National Board of Health and Welfare's own report. So why they go out in the media and report the number of dead individuals instead of deaths as a percentage of the population and claim that we had excess mortality in 2020 (which isn't true), is difficult to understand.

Susanna Hong

They want to scare us so we will go and take the injections. They use the statistics to manipulate us.

Per Eriksson

Anyone who dies within 30 days after testing positive for covid-19 is reported. Those who have died in traffic accidents or other accidents, from assault, suicide, drug abuse or anything else, are also included in the statistics on covid-19 deaths. However, those who die for the same reasons within 30 days from the time of vaccination are NOT included in the statistics on deaths due to the vaccine. On the one hand, the number of deaths in connection with covid-19 is exaggerated, on the other hand, the number of deaths in connection with covid-19 vaccinations is underestimated. One can really wonder why the authorities choose to do so.

Susanna Hong

They want to influence us so we will take the shots.

Mats Öman

There are also a lot of false positive tests due to unreliable PCR tests, which then are to form the basis for the statistics and vaccination propaganda. Biochemist and Nobel laureate Kary Mullis, who invented the technology, said himself in several interviews that PCR technology isn't a reliable test for viruses.

Alice Bäck

FHM: "The PCR technology used in tests to detect viruses cannot distinguish between viruses capable of infecting cells and viruses that have been neutralized by the immune system and therefore these tests cannot be used to determine whether someone is contagious or not."

Eva Broman

If people start dying because of the vaccinations to a greater extent, they will only blame it on a new mutation or that not everyone follows the restrictions.

Alice Bäck

During a typical flu season, hundreds of thousands of people die from the flu around the world. Mainly old and sick with weakened immune system and underlying diseases, such as diabetes, hypertension, and COPD. The flu virus becomes what tips them over the edge, so to speak, because their weak bodies can't cope with another strain. The same goes for covid-19.

Anna Westin

It isn't out of concern for "the elderly and fragile" this happens. If that will existed, healthcare would have received increased resources a long time ago. More beds, more staff, higher salaries, more education, more preventive health care, more time for the elderly, more focus on how each individual strengthens their immune system and stays as healthy as possible, feels meaningfulness, security, joy of life, community. Instead, enormous resources are now being invested in everyone being injected with emergency-approved, experimental preparations, of which no one knows the long-term effects. Who can even imagine that this is about the well-being of the elderly?

FRIDA

One of the risk factors for covid-19 is the chronic lung disease COPD. It was in the after-effects of this disease that Mum died. Mainly, it's smoking that is behind the condition, and Mum smoked for almost her whole life. The doctors explained that if you stop smoking, the disease doesn't develop in the same way. The damage that already is in the lungs in COPD can't be repaired, but the future prospects at least look better, and there are medications that can help.

But Mum never stopped smoking but took basically her last drag on her deathbed. She had probably had COPD for a long time before she was diagnosed. At first the cough, which she had had for several years, became more persistent, then she often felt out of breath and didn't have as much strength as before. She had various medications that she had to take every day, including a kind of asthma medication to facilitate breathing.

But she found it increasingly difficult to breathe, and in the end her lung capacity was so poor that she was in constant need of oxygen, and so powerless that she was nourished by tube. She lay like a little nestling in the hospital bed, gasping for air. I was so angry with her that she hadn't stopped smoking in time, even though I had appealed to her so many times, and I was completely appalled at how sick she had become. I understood that she soon would die.

Mum in the hospital bed. Mum in the coffin. The funeral. Mum's home with smoke stinking walls, furniture, carpets, curtains. Mum's belongings. The bin bags. The general cleaning. The empty apartment. The grief. The loss. The relief.

Yes, I remember that case. He was convicted in spite of his denial, wasn't he? Yes, exactly. And now he wants you to write a book about it? Yes, I don't begrudge him that. But I don't think he is innocent. If you have read the preliminary investigation, you will understand what I mean. I skimmed through it myself last week to refresh my memory a bit before the meeting with you here today. There were no circumstances whatsoever that indicated that it could be another perpetrator.

To start from the beginning, the police and an ambulance arrived at the crime scene late in the evening or early at night after a phone call from Wiklund himself to the emergency service centre. When the patrol arrived, he was standing in the gate waiting. He took the lead up to the flat where the door was ajar. One police officer, who was a woman, first became suspicious. She thought that Wiklund seemed unnaturally unaffected by the situation. But when he explained that he was a doctor, she thought that he possibly automatically took on a calm attitude and hid his feelings behind his professional role.

The situation at a crime scene can be quite chaotic when the first police patrol arrives. For example, there may be so much blood that it's difficult to endure the sight. But regardless of all the circumstances, the first patrol must secure the place. You should check if the victim is alive or not. If there is a suspected perpetrator nearby, he must be arrested immediately. You must block up and collect information and secure any traces and evidence. Of course, the responsibility should be handed over to colleagues with a higher rank as soon as possible, but in the initial stage, a heavy responsibility may rest on young, inexperienced police officers.

In the long run, no police officer can claim that he has never made a mistake at a crime scene. Making mistakes is part of human nature. But there is a difference between unintentionally breaking the rules and doing it on purpose. By this I don't mean to say that there were any serious mistakes or irregularities in this particular case, but one should be aware that the risk always exists.

The dead woman was lying on the floor in the kitchen. You saw right away that she was seriously injured and probably dead. While the paramedics and the policewoman were examining her, the policeman initiated a first interrogation with Wiklund, who then stated that he had received a phone call about twenty minutes earlier from his ex-partner, who had asked him to come to her home because she felt threatened. When he arrived at the flat, he claimed that the front door was ajar and that he found her dead on the floor in the kitchen.

Before the body was moved and transported to the institute of forensic medicine where the autopsy was to take place, forensics studied the crime scene. A forensic technician is used to entering often messy environments to secure evidence and mostly works under heavy pressure. A crime scene is time sensitive and can be damaged at any time. Every person who gets there can contaminate the tracks that could be found there.

A forensic technician is also good at reading people, and in this case, he listened together with the summoned medical examiner and a detective inspector to Wiklund's own version of the matter. I talked to my colleague later and asked for his impression of Wiklund.

Due to the further preliminary investigation, I had the opportunity to discuss the circumstances surrounding the death with the medical examiner on several occasions. I also had the opportunity to attend when the reconstruction was carried out with the ambulance personnel who were called to the scene. In connection with reviews and discussions, we also examined a number of photographs from the technical investigation.

The murder weapon was a knife, such as a bread knife, which was found in the sink. It was cleaned, and no fingerprints could be found on it, but it bore microscopic traces of the victim's blood.

The arrest hearing with Wiklund was meagre. I informed him that he was suspected of murder, and he accepted it without a word. He then had the opportunity to meet his defence councel. He didn't seem particularly frightened by the situation and didn't seem to worry about what it would mean to him in the future.

At the next interrogation, he seemed tired and dejected. My tactic is usually to start with questions about the suspect's lifestyle to get an idea of what his life looked like before the crime. What important events have occurred, what his professional and social situation looks like, what he expects from the future and so on. Then I let him reel off his story without confronting him with what we have, in order to find out how much he is willing to tell himself. In this case, I remember thinking: How is this guy going to react and act? He deviated markedly from the criminal stereotype. This was a well-educated, professional guy with a previous long-term stable relationship that also included children. He had no criminal record, and no signs of addiction or mental health problems were seen.

He had no experience of interrogation and wasn't "sit practised", as I usually say. He also had no experience of being locked up. The arrest may come as a severe shock and cause the suspect to remain silent at first, but many of the normally law-abiding type often break down within hours or days in custody and start talking.

I have investigated hundreds of serious violent crimes and only on a few occasions failed to obtain a confession. Murder is commonplace to me, but the vast majority of these murders have been committed by professional criminals or by people who have given in to greed or reckless rage.

This wasn't the case here. This guy didn't belong to the loud and aggressive type I have encountered so many times. Guys with a tendency to lean forward over the table and underline their words with their fists or wander around the room and swear or push the chair back and forth across the floor to make as much noise as possible. No, there I sat with a proper, intelligent, and dutiful type, who didn't seem the least aggressive, impulsive, or violent, and would make him talk about his feelings. There I sat, alone with him in a naked room, and would make him open up and admit a murder or manslaughter.

What strategy would I use to get emotional contact with him, and how would I set about maintaining it? How would I gain his trust and confidence? How would I demolish his defensive walls? How do you manipulate a person into doing what he wants least of all – namely, admitting to a crime that can cost him his freedom?

Everyone wants to tell their story, but not for just anyone. The listener should tolerate what he hears and not show any negative feelings, such as condemnation or distancing. Encouraging nods and a clearly shown interest usually clinch the matter when it comes to elicit confessions.

Another effective interrogation technique for eliciting revelations is to create gaps in the conversation. Almost reflexively, the suspect then fills out the void with words to break the silence.

A criminal investigator must have in-depth knowledge of human nature and different types of criminals. Logic is his main weapon, but it's ineffective if he doesn't at the same time have intuition, experience, and a willingness to get involved in the case.

An interrogation requires that all your senses work for high pressure. When you hear suspects and witnesses, you must be able to tune your emotional radar to the wavelength of truth in order to succeed in distinguishing false, jarring tones. At the same time, you must interpret facial expressions and pay attention to the slightest shift. It's important to be on the alert and not let yourself be hoodwinked. And over the years, I have talked to so many people that I can easily determine when someone is trying to throw dust in my eyes.

Murder is the most serious of all crimes and the most taboo and incomprehensible. What is it that makes a person exceed the limit?

In this case, I assumed that the perpetrator had been strongly provoked by a woman who, through her behaviour and accusations, had threatened his social and personal integrity. It turned out that Wiklund's experience of police interrogation wasn't at all as non-existent as I had hastily assumed. On the contrary, he had been in contact with the police before on several occasions due to accusations that his ex-partner had made against him. It was a motive for the murder, you could say, that she had harassed him after the separation. In addition, the couple's six-year-old daughter, who was in the flat when the murder took place, was virtually an eyewitness to the act. There was no doubt that it was Wiklund who was the perpetrator.

But he categorically stuck to his version of the course of events and firmly claimed that he was innocent. It didn't matter what I said or did. He was steadfast. Although he had pretty much everything against him, he didn't budge an inch from his statement.

THE INTERROGATION

ITR: Well, let's see, Wiklund... You have said that Sandra called you and asked for help because she felt threatened by a man.

MW: Yes.

ITR: Did she say which man it was?

MW: Yes, a man she had met at the pub.

ITR: And when was she supposed to have met that man then? The same night, or what?

MW: I don't know.

ITR: Did she say what his name was?

MW: No.

ITR: In what way did she feel threatened by him then? Did she say that?

MW: No.

ITR: But the situation was so urgent that you had to go there immediately to help her?

MW: Yes, I got the impression he was there.

ITR: That the threatening man was there, inside her flat?

MW: No, outside on the street maybe, or outside her door.

ITR: Why did she call you and not the police then?

MW: I don't know.

ITR: So, you went there. Did you think it was your duty to help her, or what?

MW: No, I thought mostly about Maja, our daughter.

ITR: You thought mostly about Maja.

MW: Yes.

ITR: Yes, because you didn't really have such a great desire to help Sandra, did you?

MW: No, maybe not.

ITR: You didn't really agree on things, did you? You were in the middle of a custody dispute, weren't you?

MW: Yes.

ITR: Still, you dropped everything you had on hand and rushed to her rescue as soon as she called you.

MW: I was worried about Maja.

ITR: Mm. And when you get there, the flat door is open, and you find Sandra dead on the floor in the kitchen.

MW: Yes.

ITR: So, this is what you have stated. But was that really what happened, Wiklund?

MW: Yes, she was dead when I got there.

ITR: We have ploughed through this a number of times now, and you continue to maintain your innocence. But if it wasn't you who killed Sandra, who did?

MW: I don't know.

ITR: Who else could have done it?

MW: I don't know.

ITR: Was there anyone else there then?

MW: No.

ITR: It was just you.

MW: Yes. But before I came, the person who killed her must have been there.

ITR: The threatening man from the pub, you mean?

MW: Yes.

ITR: You assume it was the man from the pub who killed her?

MW: Yes, it was him she felt threatened by.

ITR: That that man exists at all, we only have yours and no one else's words for.

MW: (silence)

ITR: Did you meet anyone on the stairs when you arrived?

MW: No.

ITR: Did you see anyone outside the gate?

MW: No.

ITR: On the street?

MW: No.

ITR: You heard no sound of running steps?

MW: No.

ITR: No car that started and left?

MW: No.

ITR: Come on now, Wiklund! I'm trying to give you a chance here, to come up with details that can support your statement. But you have nothing to say?

MW: No.

ITR: Well, in that case I can only express my regret. Considering your daughter's testimony... You'll be prosecuted and convicted for this, you get that, don't you?

MW: Yes, I do.

THE JUDGEMENT

To base a conviction solely on the negative fact that the investigation does not seem to leave room for any alternative perpetrator can only be considered in exceptional cases. In addition, as a rule, at least supporting evidence that clarifies the essential parts of the course of events and positively links the defendant to the crime must be required. In the present case, the investigation has not provided any support that any other possible perpetrator was at the scene when the crime was committed. Since there is also circumstantial evidence of a kind other than technical evidence, Mats Wiklund should therefore, despite the lack of direct evidence, be judged responsible for the murder of Sandra Brolin.

FRIDA

The most common method in violent crime with a fatal outcome is knife abuse. Then comes shooting, beating with or without weapon, strangulation, drowning, burning, and poisoning.

The most common motive is sudden aggression, usually in connection with the perpetrator being under the influence of alcohol or drugs.

Was that how the murder of Sandra happened? Did Mats lose his temper and stab her during an argument, as Axberg seems to believe? Sandra had reported Mats to the police for threats and assault, he said, but he hadn't been convicted of it. Why wasn't he?

Oh, I can't stand another hypocritical pile of shit! What I can't understand is why he chose me, who he knows is entirely on the side of the women, if the case is that he himself has abused a woman. I don't know what to believe. But one thing I do know. If it turns out that he belongs to the paltry group of women abusers, I want nothing more to do with him. Then there will be no book. Then he can forget all about it and fuck off.

The whole kitchen floor is bloody and in the middle of the blood the woman lies prostrate in a nasty distorted position. Her breasts and face are facing the floor and blood is flowing from her head and from the visible left half of her face. She is fully clothed. Most of the blood appears to have accumulated under her lower abdomen, as if she has suffered a miscarriage and abdominal bleeding. He may have hit and kicked her in the stomach. He may have stood up and jumped on her. One of the paramedics gently lifts her head to be able to determine through her possible eye reflexes whether she is alive or not. You can then see that her left eye is bunged up and that almost her whole face is bruised. The body is still flexible and warm but shows no signs of life. The paramedics have difficulty deciding whether to let her stay or not. If she is dead, it may be important for the police investigation that nothing is moved. On the other hand, there may be a chance that her life can be saved if she quickly receives medical care.

THE GROUP

Lars Nielsen

I'm a doctor in the ICU. About 80 % of those infected with covid-19 have mild to moderate symptoms that go away on their own. Accordingly, it mostly develops into something in between a common cold and a seasonal flu. The majority of those infected also recover. However, about 2 out of 10 get severe to critical symptoms, such as pneumonia. The infection can settle in the lungs, and those who die do so because the breathing can't oxygenate the blood, from blood poisoning, drop in blood pressure, cardiac arrest, or multiorgan failure in combination with impaired oxygenation of the blood. When organs such as the lungs, heart, liver, kidneys, and spleen lose sufficient function, death occurs.

Dag Roman

Thanks for good information, Lars. What you write reminds me of a woman who died from the vaccine. She suffered from six different life-threatening conditions almost simultaneously: massive cerebral haemorrhage, heart attack, clots in a lung, bleeding in and around the adrenal gland, heavy bleeding in the intestinal system and clots in the venous system. How was that explained?

Lars Nielsen

If I remember correctly, the hypothesis was that the vaccine had caused a condition that made the blood to start coagulating too much and that many blood clots formed at the same time in several places in the body. Eventually, massive internal bleeding occurred that led to death.

Dag Roman

And what was the reason for the vaccine causing that condition?

Lars Nielsen

I can't answer that.

Dag Roman

Do you, as a doctor, recommend getting vaccinated?

Lars Nielsen

I neither recommend nor advise against. It's up to everyone.

Dag Roman

Are you vaccinated yourself?

Lars Nielsen

I refrain from answering that question. Everyone must come to their own decision, based on the information available. I don't want to influence anyone.

Dag Roman

Okay.

Helena Widén

I have had covid. It was close that I ended up on a respirator, but I managed to avoid it at the last minute. I was hospitalized for two weeks. Now that I'm home again, I'm still very exhausted. I have difficulty breathing and feel extremely tired and weak. Before I got covid, I was offered a vaccine, but I refused because I had had a blood clot before, and I had heard that you can get clots from the vaccine. Now afterwards, when I'm still feeling unwell and I was at the health centre, they asked again if I didn't want to be vaccinated. "If you take it, you will probably feel better later." I said I have had a blood clot before and didn't want to risk getting another one. I also said that I generally don't believe in vaccines. "People get covid anyway and it doesn't protect against mutations either," I said. It's a pure poison they inject, but I didn't say that. "I won't be vaccinated no matter what you say," I said. "And now that I have had covid, I'm immune and don't need a vaccine." But they kept nagging and saying that "Pfizer is great and without side effects, so we think you should take it!" "Even though I'm immune after having covid?" I asked. "Yes, then it works all the better," they said. But I said I didn't want to and then they gave up. But they warned me and said that I would get just as sick again later without a vaccine. Not a word about everyone who gets sick DESPITE the vaccine or even FROM the vaccine. Not a word about those who have died of covid, despite the vaccine, is talked about either. And if it comes up, contrary to expectation, it's only explained away in different ways. Then an "expert" expresses an opinion and meanders and has explanations for everything, even though you know that he is just sitting there and guessing and doesn't know shit. Almost all my friends have been vaccinated and are jubilantly happy when they have received the vaccine or will soon receive it. I don't understand how they can believe that they are getting something good that helps them. I feel so strongly that I shouldn't take it, and I would feel the same way if I hadn't had a blood clot before or if I hadn't had covid, because my whole instinct tells me that the vaccine is toxic and dangerous and shouldn't enter my body.

Inger Väisänen
You who are a doctor in the ICU, Lars, may be able to describe what happens if you end up on a respirator. I've heard so many horrible stories about it.

Lars Nielsen
Because covid-19 can settle in both the upper and lower respiratory tract, there is a risk of severe shortness of breath. In the worst case, one can suffer from ARDS, acute respiratory distress syndrome, or shock lung, as it sometimes also is called. It's a life-threatening condition with oxygenation difficulties and fluid in the lungs. If this happens, a respirator treatment is started, which means that the machine takes over the breathing partially or completely.

If you are cared for with so-called invasive ventilation, you get breathing assistance via a tube that is inserted down the throat through the mouth. An alternative is to make a surgical incision in the throat and insert the tube directly into the trachea. When inserting the tube through the mouth and throat, the patient must be so deeply anesthetized that all consciousness is gone. If you have a weak heart, it can be affected so that it risks stopping.

In addition to being anesthetized, you also get muscle relaxants for the vocal cords to relax so much that the tube gets past them and can be brought down. This means that you can't talk when connected to the respirator. You are also treated with analgesic morphine preparations.

Almost all are anesthetized at least the first few days on the respirator. Later, you can get lighter doses of soporific, which means you can be relatively awake.

A respirator treatment is never stopped abruptly, but you usually slowly reduce the pressure and the amount of oxygen that the machine provides. The patient must breathe more and more of his own power to train his respiratory muscles again. Even before the respirator is disconnected, the patient is also to do physiotherapy, such as lifting arms and legs. It's called "out training", that is the patient trains out of the machine.

A respirator treatment is always a great strain on the body, and some don't survive. This is especially true for elderly, fragile people and people suffering from heart failure or severe COPD.

Inger Väisänen
Many thanks, Lars.

Ulf Johansson
I've been on a respirator, so I know how it feels. It's certainly not the same for everyone, but for me it was a nightmare. At the same time, I am very grateful that the doctors kept me alive and managed to wake me up again.

It started with coughing and pressure over my chest in March last year. It got worse with each passing day, and after a week I went to the emergency room. Then I had such poor oxygenation that I quite immediately was put on a respirator.

Then I found myself in a constant nightmare-like state where dreams were mixed with reality, and I felt a terrible anxiety. Sometimes I was aware that I was being washed and turned and that they changed my diaper, but most of the time I thought I was under the surface in a water-filled closed tank that I couldn't get out of. There was a minimal air pocket at the top under the lid that I could breathe in if I pressed my head against the lid as much as I could. It was probably a mental picture of my physical condition that my brain created when I was lying there fighting for my life, but the feeling was, to put it bluntly, fucking awful.

When I woke up after a week, at first I didn't know where I was. I couldn't move my head and arms and thought I was tied to the bed. My wife, who was sitting next to me, I thought was a prison guard who would make sure I didn't escape. I had oxygen in my nose and holes in my throat and shunts in my arms, but I didn't become aware of that until later.

I survived, but I still don't feel well. I'm extremely sensitive to sound and light and I don't have as much energy as before. The brain also doesn't function as before. I lose words and have difficulty concentrating. But I survived, and that's the main thing. I can't thank enough the medical team who saved my life.

Inger Väisänen
Many thanks to you too, Helena and Ulf, who shared your experiences.

FRIDA

Maja Brolin has agreed to meet me. Mats gave me her grand-father's e-mail address, and I sent him an e-mail asking him to present my question and explanation to Maja. She got my e-mail address and could choose to answer me or not. She is still underage, and it was perhaps wrong of me to contact her considering that her grandmother according to Mats doesn't want her to be involved with him again, but her grandfather isn't against it, and therefore I thought I could do it. After all, it's her dad it's about, and I think she has the right to choose for herself what she wants to do when it comes to him.

  – *I don't want to meet Dad anymore.*

    – *You don't?*

    – *No.*

    – *Why not?*

    – *He is weird.*

    – *In what way is he weird?*

    – *Don't know. Just weird.*

    – *Yes, then you can tell him you don't want to.*

    – *Can't you do it instead?*

    – *Yes, but then he might think that it's me who wants it that way. It's better that you do it yourself, Frida.*

    – *He will get angry.*

    – *You can say it on the phone next time he calls.*

    – *Yes, and when he gets angry, I just hang up.*

I was only six years old when Dad went to prison. I haven't met him since. Grandma told me that it wouldn't be good for me to see him in prison and that he had no right to see me considering what he had done. He had forfeited that right forever, she said.

But I thought about him sometimes and couldn't be angry with him though I knew he had killed Mum. I longed for him and wanted him to be with me. But at last, it was as if he didn't exist and had never existed. Nobody talked about him at home, so I almost forgot him.

I know he will soon have served his sentence and will come out. I got help from a friend's mum to find out, and I think about him quite a lot now. I haven't told Grandma that I know because she has always been so negative towards him. And that's not so strange since he killed her daughter. Of course, she can't forgive him for that.

But I can forgive him for killing my mum, because I don't think it was his intention to do it. I think Mum quarrelled with him so he lost patience and couldn't control himself.

Because it was always Mum who started arguing. She was the one who was disorderly and got angry first. I remember that. Dad was always so calm and patient.

But he killed her. I didn't see exactly when it happened, but I saw her afterwards when she was lying on the floor in the kitchen, and he stood leaning over her with the knife in his hand and when he went to the sink and rinsed it off. He didn't see me until I asked what he was doing.

I woke up to Mum screaming. She was angry and shouted. Then it went quiet, and I fell asleep again, I think. At first,

I didn't know that it was Dad who was there, that it was he who had come to us, but then I heard his voice when he talked to Mum and she answered. Then there was no more quarrelling, so I heard their voices only faintly. I thought it sounded like Mum was sad and crying. Then it went quiet again, and I got up and saw Dad with the knife in his hand. I remember asking him what he had done to Mum, and I remember he said I should go back to my room, and after a while he came in to me and said that there had been an accident with Mum and that I had to go to Aunt Birgitta, who lived next to us. He said that Mum was already dead when he came to us. But I heard her voice and that he was talking to her, and I told the police. When I said to Dad before, that I had heard Mum's voice, he said I must have dreamed it, but I knew I hadn't.

Just because Dad said I was wrong, I thought about it a lot afterwards. I kind of didn't want to give in. I went through it in my mind and decided that it must have been just as I remembered it and not as Dad said it was. Maybe that's why I still remember it so well.

I also remember that I was interrogated, and that what we said was recorded on video, but I don't remember what it was like. I don't remember what questions I got or what I felt when I was sitting there. I just answered without thinking, I suppose. For example, I didn't think about what it would be like for Dad because of what I said. I don't think I was shocked either because I never really saw Mum when she was lying on the floor. If she was bloody and looked horrible when she was dead, I never saw it with my own eyes, because Dad took me away from there immediately when I came out of my room.

When you are six years old, you don't understand much, but now that I'm older, I think that Dad might have avoided prison if I hadn't told the police as it was. If I had kept quiet, I mean. I hadn't needed to lie, but I could have refrained from telling and answering the questions I was asked. Maybe I could have saved him.

But he killed Mum, and then it was probably right that he was punished for it. He told me it wasn't him, but who else could it have been? It was just him and Mum there. I heard their voices before, and I saw both of them afterwards.

Sometimes I think I would like to meet him and ask why he did it. Now that I'm not little anymore, Grandma can't stop me. But I don't know if I dare.

THE DIALOGUE

FRIDA: I have met Maja now. She gave me permission to tell you everything she told me.

MATS: Oh, you have met her?

FRIDA: Yes, we met in the park, where you and I usually meet, and kept our distance.

MATS: Yes, I don't think that you... How is she? How is she doing?

FRIDA: She seems to be fine.

MATS: What did she say?

FRIDA: She knows that you will soon leave prison and said that she would like to meet you but doesn't know if she dares.

MATS: She remembers me anyway?

FRIDA: Yes, she does. And she forgives you for what she thinks you did to Sandra.

MATS: Did she say that?

FRIDA: Yes.

MATS: What does she remember of what happened?

FRIDA: She said that she heard you and Sandra talking just before.

MATS: Yes, she thought so. But she must have dreamed it.

FRIDA: Dreamed?

MATS: Yes. Sandra was already dead when I got there.

FRIDA: She also said that you and Sandra quarrelled quite a lot.

MATS: Yes, we did.

FRIDA: And that it was usually Sandra who started.

MATS: Did she say that?

FRIDA: Yes, and that you might have gotten so angry with her that you lost control and killed her by mistake.

MATS: She thinks it was an accident?

FRIDA: Yes. She saw you with the knife in your hand afterwards and asked what you had done.

MATS: Yes.

FRIDA: You held the knife in your hand?

MATS: No, it was in the sink, and I never touched it.

FRIDA: Why did Maja say that you held it in your hand then?

MATS: She must have imagined it based on what she thought had happened.

FRIDA: Okay. But it's true that you and Sandra often quarrelled?

MATS: Yes.

FRIDA: She reported you to the police for threats and assault?

MATS: Yes, that's right.

FRIDA: Tell me about the reports.

MATS: Haven't you read the preliminary investigation and the judgement?

FRIDA: No, I want to hear it from you first.

MATS: Why?

FRIDA: I don't want to be influenced by what the authorities arrived at. I want to feel that I can trust you.

MATS: How are you going to achieve that then?

FRIDA: By asking you and sensing how it feels when you answer.

MATS: Feel if I'm lying or not?

FRIDA: Yes. So now I ask: Did you abuse Sandra?

MATS: No, I didn't.

FRIDA: Why did she report you to the police then?

MATS: I want you to form your own opinion about that through what you learn from others than me.

FRIDA: Yeah, okay.

FRIDA

I was paying attention to his voice the whole time. A raised voice mode is almost always a sign of lying because lies trigger an emotional reaction that causes the vocal cords to contract. If you know the phenomenon, which Mats certainly does, you can of course deliberately control the voice mode so that it stays where you want it.

Another sign of lying is that you take a break before answering since it's a mental challenge to lie. But Mats showed no signs of telling lies. The only thing I perceived was a slight shift in his charisma when he said that he never held the knife, and that Maja must have dreamed that she heard him talking to Sandra. Did he lie there? His voice mode didn't change, and he answered without hesitation, but he kept his head down and didn't look at me when he answered.

And it doesn't make sense. Why would Maja imagine that Mats was holding a knife in his hand and think that he had injured Sandra with it, if the knife was in the sink the whole time so she couldn't see it? He said that what she claimed must be a rationalization, but that isn't credible.

I could have asked questions and pressured him, but I didn't. It's difficult to maintain a lie if you are subjected to a detailed questioning. Especially if it's a spontaneous and ill-considered lie. Few people are quick-witted enough to be able to come up with credible and sustainable explanations in an instant if the lie is being questioned.

But I didn't pressure him. It's too early for that, and I don't want to risk him losing trust in me and perhaps withdraw.

I was watching TV when Mats came and rang the doorbell. I didn't know what time it was, but I opened the door, because I thought it was Sandra who came. She used to look in sometimes when she had been out having fun.

But it was Mats, and he had the little girl with him. "There has been an accident and I need to call the police and an ambulance," he said. "Can Maja sleep here tonight?" And that was all right with me because she had done that many times before. "What has happened?" I said. "Is it Sandra?" "Yes, it's Sandra," he said. I thought it was strange that he hadn't already called for help. If she was so ill that she needed to be picked up by an ambulance, shouldn't that have been the first thing he did? But I didn't ask because he looked so resolute that I didn't dare. And I didn't want to ask Maja not to worry her. But of course I wondered.

Sandra and I weren't close, so I didn't really know much about her, other than that she was out and enjoyed herself quite often after the separation from Mats. That's why I often had Maja with me at night. I always got paid, so I can't complain about that, but it felt a little uncomfortable considering the girl that she drank and brought strangers home from the pub. I really thought so. But it was none of my business, and it can't be so easy to be left like that when you are still young and on the alert. It was sad for both her and Maja that Mats moved out. Maja said so sometimes, that she longed for her dad. She met him, but of course that wasn't the same as having him living with her.

Mats was so calm and nice, and I had such a hard time grasping that it was he who had killed Sandra when I once found out that was the case. He had always made a very sympathetic impression on me. That evening, when he came and rang the doorbell and left Maja, would he have shortly before stabbed Sandra to death? Consequently, while he was here, standing and talking to me, Sandra lay dead in the apartment. If she had still been alive, he would of course have called an ambulance before he came to me.

But shouldn't it have been noticed by his manner that he had lost his temper and killed her? Shouldn't he have been upset and afraid or shocked and confused? But he was very calm. Calm and as *determined,* I thought, as if he knew exactly what he was doing. And he was a doctor and probably used to dealing with difficult situations.

The woman shows signs of medical shock. The pulse is fast and weak, the breathing shallow, the lips bluish, and the skin pale grey and cold sweaty. Her jeans are bloody and have a large tear above one knee. I make the tear bigger and see that blood wells up from a deep wound in her leg. I compress the wound edges, press against the wound and lift the leg up against a stump so that it ends up above the level of the heart to lower the blood pressure right where the injury is. I fold her cap and put it over the wound. To create a constant pressure, I place a thick stick on top and tie her scarf around it to attach the device. It continues to bleed, and I take her belt and tighten it around her thigh to limit the blood supply. It's a temporary measure. After half an hour, there is a risk that the tissue in the damaged body part will suffer from a lack of oxygen, and this can cause permanent damage.

FRIDA

There is so much in this that arouses memories. I never know when it will happen or what may trigger it. Suddenly there is just a flash of a memory in my brain, and I am back in a situation and in an emotional state that I have been in before.

My brain feels rather overloaded right now. In addition to being on the alert at work, I listen to, and try to assess, different people's statements in connection with the book, and in my spare time I collect information about the pandemic and the vaccines to be able to decide whether I should get vaccinated or not. It's interesting to read what people think and feel, and it's good to get information from different sources, but I still have to make my own assessment of all the facts and theories to arrive at what's right for me.

FACEBOOK

Sylvia Brundin
What do you think about the Roll Up campaign?
Personally,I think it's both insulting and unethical!

Karin Blomgren
It's approved by both the Swedish Public Health Agency
and the Swedish Civil Contingencies Agency.

Folke Hjelm
Yes, they seem to have a mutual hidden agenda.

Nina Söderblom
It's an agenda where the state renames a bad seasonal
flu to a pandemic to get people mass vaccinated.

Sylvia Brundin
How can talented artists and other celebrities support
this? I quote: "We are not just rolling up to keep
ourselves healthy. We also do it for each other. Get
vaccinated when it's your turn. Who are we talking
to? We want to influence those who for one reason or
another feel uncertain. As human beings, we all strive for
community and belonging. When we are hesitant
about something, or when we feel that the choice isn't
so important – it may be to choose vegetarian meat but
also a certain brand among several – we tend to follow
the majority. Therefore, our campaign shows how the
majority stand up for each other in the vaccine issue."

Folke Hjelm
Yes, there they really reveal what psychological
mechanisms they benefit from.

Tomas Bergman
Most people would rather belong to the majority than do the right thing.

Sylvia Brundin
To the initiators and celebrities and all other gullible and irresponsible people who participate in this stunt, I want to say: Unsure people should be given comprehensive and objective information, not deliberately be affected in a certain direction. When it comes to community and belonging, you of course join a group that has the same values as yourself and not just any group just because a number of celebrities do so. Yes, dependent and unsure individuals may follow the majority, but certainly not those with strong integrity who think freely and independently. And those who believe that they can be vaccinated out of solidarity haven't taken in relevant information. Vaccinated people become infected with covid-19 and can infect others. And some who have been vaccinated suffer from symptoms that the vaccine should actually have protected against. The hidden statistics when it comes to side effects of the vaccines are large.

Regina Madsen
That through massive pressure in the media, almost scare people into "obedience" makes me suspect that this is about something else than protecting people's lives and health.

Ylva Borén
Yes, I don't want to be part of an experiment where people are incited to take an untested so-called vaccine

against a virus whose mortality is below one percent if you are not old and frail. I wouldn't take the shots even if I got a million.

Lennart Lindh
Amazing how many fact-resistant foil hats are attracted by this.

Regina Madsen
I feel it's not right. There is something going on behind the scenes that we are not allowed to know.

Folke Hjelm
The authorities have teamed up with party fixers and celebrities to push the flock of sheep into the vaccine booth by hook or by crook.

Åsa Westerberg
Instead of vaccinating against covid-19, you should reduce the risk of becoming infected by preventing with, for example, vitamin D. It is proven that vitamin D levels are decisive for the risk of being affected.

Tanja Wik
And if you eat a vegetarian diet, you are 73 % less likely to get seriously ill with covid-19, according to a study published in the British Medical Journal.

Nina Söderblom
It's also possible to both prevent and treat covid-19 with certain proven drugs and medications. That you don't do this is because the pharmaceutical companies don't make that much money on those preparations. However, they make billions on vaccines. For example, they don't

want to hear about Ivermectin, because this drug, which has already been used by millions of people and is completely harmless in recommended doses, doesn't have its patent left, which means that everyone can manufacture it at low cost and no one can make money on it.

Björn Hansson
Ivermectin is a drug normally used to deworm livestock.

Nina Söderblom
Among many other things. It's used on both humans and animals.

Kajsa Bishop
The pharmaceutical companies are investing in preventive drugs such as blood pressure medication and blood lipid lowering medications, which they can make humanity take for decades and make extremely much money on. This also applies to the covid-19 vaccines.

Leif Nylander
The vaccine wasn't developed for Covid-19, but Covid-19 was developed for the vaccine. The power elite wants to depopulate the world with POISON VACCINES. That's why everyone should be vaccinated as soon as possible. It's all about getting as many people as possible to take the deadly POISON in the shortest possible time. People will die like flies in the next two years. Just wait and see... Why vaccinate people if it isn't needed? Why force people to have a POISON cocktail that no pharma-ceutical company can guarantee a safe outcome with? The pandemic is made up. Covid-19 doesn't exist! Just the usual seasonal flu that every year kills

people over the age of 80 who already have underlying diseases and who get morphine so the heart stops. Covid-19 is HUMBUG straight through. It's with SCAREMONGERING that the authorities want us to OBEY in order to create a totalitarian world order where the MAFFIA rules with FASCIST methods. So think carefully before you take this POISON VACCINE that has already killed thousands of people, because afterwards you can actually NOT REGRET! I am absolutely convinced that you are facing a life-changing decision! So think carefully if you want to live and stay for a while longer on this wonderful planet!

I was shocked when the police called and told me that my daughter was dead and that I had to come and pick up Maja at the neighbour's wife. I couldn't take it in. I knew that Mats had started abusing her, but that it would go so far as to kill her I could never have believed. She sometimes showed me the bruises she had gotten when he had pushed and hit her. It was a relief that he moved so that she didn't have to feel threatened and afraid anymore, I thought. It was better for Maja too, to be spared from seeing her mum get   beaten.

But the worst happened some time later. Then he came close to killing her. Then he hit her so badly that she had to seek medical attention. She had never had to do that before. And she had never reported him to the police, but after that attack, she finally did. He denied it and accused her of making a false statement, which of course wasn't true. And there were witnesses, she told me, so he wouldn't get away with it.

I don't know how it turned out, because she didn't want to talk about it, and I'm not the one to nag. She had a couple of girlfriends she trusted, and that was enough for her, I suppose. The only thing I know is that she was hit in the head and got remaining injuries from it in the form of migraine attacks.

Considering everything I knew about Mats' treatment of her, I wasn't really surprised when it turned out that he had killed her. I just never thought it would go that far. But behind the calm and polite surface, he was erratic and violent. Not many people knew about it, or wanted to believe it, even though there was evidence. He deceived those around him with his polite and proper facade.

It turned out that Maja had virtually witnessed the murder. When the police interrogation with her was over, and she had come to us, I asked a little cautiously what had happened when her mum died. "It was Dad who stabbed her with a knife," she said. There wasn't much more I could get out of her. I wanted to help her forget it, so I didn't persist. When she asked for her dad, I said that he was in prison and that children weren't allowed to come and visit. I lied to protect her.

For my own part I didn't intend to visit him after all the harm he had done to our daughter. If he had admitted and explained himself and shown that he was sad and felt remorse, I might have felt differently, but he denied everything and didn't in any way reveal what he felt. I thought that was cowardly. I still think so. Pathetic and cowardly, as if trying to convince himself that it had never happened. As if Sandra was insignificant and not worth remembering.

How could he deny that he was guilty, when even his own daughter knew it and said so? As if she wasn't worth listening to and believing in either. But she was there and saw it! And fortunately, the police believed her, even though what she told them wasn't decisive for the outcome. She was only six years old, and you can't attach too much importance to what such a young child says, but of course it would have felt better for her if her dad had at least confirmed that she had perceived the situation correctly. Indirectly, he instead claimed that she had misunderstood it all or even lied! No, he said she must have dreamed what she saw and heard. He tried to get her to start doubting her senses. I get so terribly upset when I think of it! How he sacrificed his own child in an attempt

64

to save his own skin. Fortunately, it didn't succeed.

And soon he will have served his sentence and atoned for his crime, as they so prettily put it. Soon he will be out again. I really hope he doesn't try to contact us then. That he has a sense of decency enough not to look us up.

I haven't told Maja that he will soon be free. I don't want her to be involved with him again. But if he wants to meet her, and she agrees, I can't stop him, I guess. And what is this idea he has gotten that a book should be written about him? What should that book contain? Even more lies? Or is he just out to make money?

The grief for Sandra was difficult for us to bear. Her father probably mourned as much as I did, but for him it was expressed in a completely different way. I needed to talk about Sandra and my grief. I needed a person who could listen to me. I understand that it isn't the same for everyone, but I had a need to share what I felt to be able to move on. I had a friend who didn't let me down, but many of our acquaintances seemed to be afraid of me after Sandra had died. Some chose the easiest way, which was to avoid me. Neighbours I had talked to quite a lot before greeted me only distantly and embarrassedly on the stairs. It felt sad, but I understand that death is frightening and that it can be difficult to know how to behave towards a person who is grieving.

Inside me it's cold and empty. There is no crying. I cannot breathe. The weight over my chest is suffocating me. Help me, help me, I think, but I don't say it. No one can help me. The whole burden of shock, sorrow, and despair I must shoulder myself and be able to bear.

FRIDA

Carina seems happier now that she no longer has to come to work heavily made up and with scarves wrapped around her neck to hide the bruises after his strangleholds. He got two years, so he will soon be out again, but she has promised herself not to let him come back, she says. Well, we haven't seen that yet, I think, because I know how it usually goes, but I don't voice my doubts out loud. She may be able to do it, even though he is the worst kind of asshole that surely won't let himself be fobbed off so easily.

It wasn't for the assault he was convicted, but for other crimes. She has never dared to report him for fear that the children will be taken from her.

This is what she says in my book: "Kristoffer and I have been together for four years and we have a three-year-old son together. I have a five-year-old daughter from a previous relationship. We have always quarrelled a lot, because we are both hot-tempered, but when he lost his job, he became restless and extra annoyed and started calling me ugly things for no reason. I was constantly accused of being unfaithful. I avoided meeting my mum because he accused me of sleeping with her partner. I couldn't meet my sister because, according to Kristoffer, she was a whore. I was called a whore myself if I came home late or if a guy looked at me.

I think Kristoffer needs help. He doesn't feel well from going unemployed and has started drinking more than he did before. He isn't as aggressive when he is sober, but he is controlling and jealous then too, and he has always had an easy time losing his temper. He has beaten me many times. I have started photographing the injuries, but I haven't been on sick leave because it feels like a relief for me to go to work.

Once when he was angry and started throwing spiteful remarks at me, he called me into the kitchen. I stood by the stove with my back to him, and suddenly I got a fist blow on the left side of my face. Then he grabbed my upper arms and shook me. I don't remember what we said. The children were at home and ran in and out of the balcony. I think I had been out on the balcony smoking and then going inside. I don't remember how it ended. I don't think the children noticed what was happening. It wasn't loud.

The blow hurt and I got bruises on my face and arms. I took pictures of the injuries because I was tired of him hitting me all the time. I photographed my face immediately afterwards and my arms a few days later. I had pain in my left ear for several weeks. It was a tiny bruise, so I thought it was strange that it hurt so much. But I put on make-up and went to work as usual.

Another time when we were arguing, I told him he had to move. Then he came up to me and hit me in the head with his fist. It was in the doorway to the kitchen. The blow hurt a lot and made my nose start bleeding. I didn't understand how it could hurt so much, but a few days later he told me that he had a snuff box in his hand when he walloped me. I was in pain for several weeks.

On another occasion when I was sitting in bed and it had been fussy for several days about Felicia's dad, he came in and wanted to talk to me. He grabbed my right index finger and bent it up. It hurt so much that I screamed straight out and said that my finger would come off if he didn't stop. Then he let go, but I couldn't use my finger properly for a month.

Another time he punched me in the face. I turned blue

67

under the eye and got like an abscess on my cheek. In the evening when I was going to put Robin to bed, he happened to touch the boil, and it felt like it was cracking under my skin.

I was home with the kids because they were both sick. We were lying on the couch and watching a movie. Kristoffer showered and seemed calm. Robin was grumpy and started arguing, and Kristoffer came out of the bathroom and was mad at me because he thought I treated Robin differently to how I treat Felicia. He punched me in the face and hit me on the right cheek. Then he started tearing my hair and hitting me in the face. I don't know how many blows it was. I asked him to stop because the children were there, but he just turned around and gave me a hard blow to the head. I fell to the floor but quickly got up again. The blow hurt terribly. It felt like he had smashed my head. I ran to a mirror but saw nothing unusual. I had been waiting to get the blow that would make me one of the women you read about in the newspapers, and that evening it came. I thought I would be killed or injured for life. But I didn't dare to contact the police, because among other things, I was afraid that the social services would take charge of the children if it became clear in what state our family was."

- *Why did you marry Sören, Mum?*
  - *Because I was in love with him.*
  - *Are you still in love with him?*
  - *Yes, I am.*
  - *But he just drinks and fights.*
  - *It's not that often, honey. And he is kind when he is sober.*
  - *But he is dead disgusting when he is drunk! And he beats us.*

– Yes, he mustn't do that.

– But he does!

– Mm.

– My dad never hit me.

– No, he didn't. But Frida? You mustn't tell anyone what Sören does when he is drunk. Can you promise me that? Otherwise, the authorities may decide that you and your brother can't live here anymore. Do you understand?

– Mm.

Sandra and I were workmates and best friends. We had been for a long time. When she and Mats became a couple, she was very happy. He was so understanding and loving, she said. I met him a few times, but we never saw each other all three together. I never got to know him very well.

He beat her, but at that time I didn't know. After the incident in the parking garage, which happened after he had moved, she came to my home and told me everything. She came straight from the health centre then, and she showed me what a terrible bruise she had gotten on one arm.

It was a Saturday, and Maja was with her grandmother. At nine o'clock when Sandra came down to the garage in order to take her car to go shopping, Mats was standing there waiting for her. He was angry and wanted to talk with her about Maja. Suddenly he grabbed her and pushed her up against a concrete pillar and pounded her head against it several times. She fainted and must have fallen from upright straight down onto the concrete floor.

When she woke up, she was bloody in her face. Her nose was bleeding, and there was blood on the floor and on her clothes. She didn't know why she was bleeding, but she believed that she had fallen to the side and perhaps hit both her nose and arm on the floor.

When she woke up, a man was standing next to her, and he helped her up and asked how she felt. She had seen him before in the garage but didn't know who he was. She said she had to go up to her flat, and he followed her up in the elevator and to her door. Then he went down again.

When she came in and looked at the clock, she saw that it

was over ten, and she couldn't believe that she had been un-conscious for so long. She thought it could be serious and that she needed to be examined by a doctor. She had a head-ache and a large bump in the back of her head and was com-pletely bruised on her right arm.

She washed herself and changed clothes and went to the health centre. She told the doctor that she had been beaten and that she would report it to the police.

When she was done at the doctor's, she called me and asked if she could come. She didn't dare to be home alone if she had suffered a brain injury and might faint again. At the health centre, she had received a reassuring message, but she didn't really dare to trust it.

I gave her tea and took care of her, and she told me what had happened. It wasn't the first time Mats had maltreated her, she said, but she had never reported him to the police before. Once he had threatened her with a knife and cut her in the head while she was asleep so the whole bed had be-come bloody. When I asked why she hadn't reported him to the police that time, she said that it happened while she was expecting Maja and that she didn't want him to end up in prison so she would be left alone with the child.

A few days after the assault in the garage, she said she had seen the man who helped her up in the elevator sitting in a car on the street outside her house. She hadn't approached him, but she had written down the car's registration number and handed it to the police.

It's so inconceivable and horrible that she was beaten. She didn't tell me anything while it was going on, and I didn't suspect anything. It wasn't until afterwards, when he had left her, that I was told. She protected him to the very last. But she "had plans," she said. On reporting him, I assumed, but I didn't ask, because she seemed reluctant to talk about it. She was perhaps afraid that he would contact me and ask me if he began to suspect that she was about to debunk him, I thought. I knew *nothing* then, about how it would develop and that it would end with her death.

The man is lying flat on the cement floor in the garage with the right part of his forehead pressed against the ground, and in that position, he has been hit by very strong force to the head. On his bloody skull you can see marks of both the toe area and the heel of a rough-rifled boot. The parietal bone has been displaced during the assault, so the head must have rested against a solid surface while the perpetrator with reckless force trampled, stomped, and kicked him to death.

THE DIALOGUE

MATS: A police investigator called and announced that I was suspected of a crime and was to appear for questioning. I was told that I was suspected of threatening and abusing Sandra. She had suffered a head injury that was so serious that she had had to see a doctor. He further said that there were witness statements and surveillance footage that substantiated the suspicion against me, and that I needed a public defence councel.

FRIDA: But what she accused you of wasn't true.

MATS: No, it wasn't.

FRIDA: She claimed that you had abused her before as well.

MATS: Yes, and that wasn't true either.

FRIDA: On one occasion you had cut her in the head with a knife, she told her best friend.

MATS: I see.

FRIDA: Why do you think she said that?

MATS: I don't know.

FRIDA: But what did you think about it?

MATS: I don't know. I suppose she wanted to… No, I don't

know. In fact, it was she who stabbed *me.*

FRIDA: She did?

MATS: Yes.

FRIDA: Tell me what happened.

MATS: How can you believe me when it's impossible to verify? It will just seem like I'm throwing the blame on someone else.

FRIDA: No. I always try to listen openly and unconditionally.

MATS: Yes, it was when she was expecting Maja. She was in her seventh month and had been emotionally unstable for almost the whole pregnancy. One night when I was on my way to the bedroom, she came towards me with a knife in her hand. The tip of the knife pointed at me at stomach level. The first thing she did was to cut with the knife in the air. It wasn't an aggressive movement, and I had time to take a step back, but if I hadn't moved backwards, I would have got the knife in me.

Then she held the knife to her own stomach and said she would "rip it up and take the baby out". She looked weird, and I tried to get her to drop the knife, which she eventually did. When I asked why she had threatened with the knife, she didn't seem to understand what I meant. She was just going to put it away so that no one could take it, she said. She didn't seem to remember what she had done and behaved as if nothing had happened.

In the middle of the night, I woke up and saw her standing by the window. I could only see her silhouette. I felt that my face was wet, and I didn't understand what it was, so I got up and went to the bathroom and looked at myself in the mirror. Then I saw that I had a several centimetres long bleeding wound in my head. It didn't hurt, but it was bleeding, and I tried to stop the blood flow by pressing a towel against the wound.

When I looked into the bedroom, Sandra had turned on the light and was removing the bedding from my bed. I tried to talk to her, but she seemed absent and confused and didn't answer. After a while, she came out with my sheets in her arms and said she would go to the laundry room.

I cleaned the wound, which wasn't very deep and had stopped bleeding, and washed myself. When Sandra came back, I asked her why she had used the knife against me. Then she said that she didn't remember it and that she must have done it in her sleep. She had dreamed of a knife that she had to put away so that no one would be harmed, she said.

Somnambulism is a well-established sleep disorder, but it's very rare in adults and Sandra had never shown any signs of having that disorder. I didn't know if she was lying or if she didn't actually remember.

FRIDA: What did you do then?

MATS: Nothing.

FRIDA: You didn't report it to the police?

MATS: No, I didn't. I thought she needed help, and that I could help her myself. And she was seven months pregnant, so how would that have turned out?

FRIDA: She threatened you with a knife and stabbed you and you just let it pass?

MATS: I understand that it may seem strange. But what happened that day and night were two so unreal events that I couldn't take it really seriously. Nothing like that had happened before and nothing similar happened later either. It was just an absurd parenthesis, which didn't belong to our ordinary life.

FRIDA: What did you think as a doctor about her behaviour?

MATS: I attributed it to her condition, I think. That she was pregnant. Hormones can mess up a lot. Before she became pregnant, she also had quite severe PMS symptoms, in the form of mood swings, affect lability and sleep disorders.

FRIDA: Affect lability?

MATS: Yes, or to put it more simply: She became anxious, depressed, irritable, and aggressive.

FRIDA: It must have been hard for both her and you.

MATS: Yes, it was. But I learned to recognize it and tried not to react too personally to it.

FRIDA: Mm.

MATS: Maybe that's why I took it easier than I should have done when she stabbed me. But you who are... who see it from the outside, might think I should have done more.

FRIDA: No, I know how it can be.

THE GROUP

Ivan Sköld
It isn't easy to find information about, for example, side effects of the vaccines. The information is censored everywhere. Questioning posts are mocked, and vaccine sceptics are branded as foil hats. Groups that discuss side effects are shut down and have to move to other platforms, such as this one. Instead of critically examining the state and the authorities, they attack those who warn.

Per Eriksson
Agree. The authorities' registers for reported side effects of medicines are a pure jungle to search in. Nowhere is a linking and matching of the worldwide reported side effects of covid vaccines going on, and some countries don't even have a system for reporting.

Sara Neumann
Yep, that's how it is. The questioning voices, including Nobel laureates and other prominent doctors and researchers such as Michael Yeadon, former CEO and Chief Scientist at Pfizer, jeopardize their reputation, their professional career, and their livelihood by appearing and commenting on the risks of the vaccines, and they are censored or dismissed as nutcases. But for what reason would all these wise and eminent men have suddenly become nutcases?

Christina Samuelsson
They may seem credible and convincing, but when they start talking about global conspiracies, at least I am losing confi-

dence in them. Who would be behind that agenda and for what reason would they want control over everything?

Sara Neumann

We are fed with vaccine propaganda around the clock. I think we need balance in all the information from the mainstream media. Right now, there is a total imbalance. Only one side gets space in the media and there is no public debate. Critical and factual articles are rejected, and knowledgeable, well-educated people are censored, persecuted, and violated by authorities and private individuals. It's unacceptable and a threat to free speech and democracy. Censorship is the first sign of dictatorship.

Philip Gardner

"The further a society drifts from the truth, the more it will hate those that speak it." (George Orwell)

Sara Neumann

"Visit the Covid-19 Information Centre for more help and information about vaccines." This link appears on Facebook during each post that contains the word vaccine and/or the word covid-19. By clicking on the link, "correct" information is provided and the only "truth" accepted by the authorities, which can't be questioned under any circumstances. Therefore, one must now misspell and code the words in order not to risk being censored or suspended.

Ylva Borén

Yes, it's deplorable to say the least! As if you are automatically classified as a blockhead and must be taught the only "right thing" as soon as you express an opinion on this topic!

Philip Gardner
"Truth doesn't mind being questioned. A lie doesn't like being challenged."

Per Eriksson
On 27 January 2021, the Council of Europe signed a resolution stating that vaccinations in the Member States must not be mandatory. It also states: "No one may be discriminated against for not having been vaccinated due to possible health risks, or because the person simply doesn't want to be vaccinated. Source: Council of Europe: Resolution 2361. That resolution is already being violated.

Ylva Borén
It's incomprehensible that the general public accepts the lack of comprehensive information and obediently queues for a vaccine that is only emergency approved. The so-called vaccines are in fact insufficiently explored substances whose long-term effects we know nothing about. Internationally, more and more doctors and scientists are protesting against this gigantic experiment on humanity.

Jenny Hultén
Yes, they must fight against all the authorities, organizations and politicians who are responsible and are there to protect the population and protect people's lives and health.

Mattias Svedjeholm
On 20 May, it was announced that the EU Member States

and the European Parliament have reached a joint agreement on "digital covid certificates", which will apply from the first of July. Is that to protect the population? I don't think so. What kind of society do we get with vaccine passes? It will lead us towards a totalitarian society where the state controls every citizen down to the smallest detail. Is that really how we want it?

Jenny Hultén

I have no theory about what may be behind the authorities' actions, but it feels very scary, I think. I've felt that way all along, ever since the persuasions began. Why do we have to be persuaded?

Mattias Svedjeholm

Compulsory vaccination and vaccination passes are not only undemocratic and offensive to the individual and to public health in general, all coercion (including indirect coercion through persuasion, pressure, and threats) is also contrary to the Nuremberg Convention.

Jenny Hultén

I found this, but I don't know where it comes from.
"The patient's right to self-determination is a guiding principle in social and health care. According to the Patient Act, care and treatment must be given in agreement with the patient. The principle emphasizes voluntariness in seeking care or clientele and in agreeing to various care and other measures. The right to self-determination means that the patient has the right to participate in the decision-making that applies to himself. An action or intervention concerning health

can only be carried out if the person in question has given his or her consent of his or her own free will and with knowledge of all the circumstances that affect the decision. The patient also has the right to refuse to follow decisions that may harm his own health or life and the right to refuse to receive planned or already initiated care or treatment. Those who participate in the care must respect the patient's own decisions."

Mattias Svedjeholm
Thanks, Jenny.

Anna Westin
I have worked in healthcare throughout my working life. In the 80's, when I was placed in an infection clinic, we had patients who came in with pneumonia, meningitis, killer bacteria, hepatitis, the common childhood diseases and much more, and we had patients who came home with various tropical diseases that we didn't always even know what they were. I have cared for more people than I can count. I have cared for babies, school children, young, old. Many we saved, others not. Following all those who came in with, for example, HIV, and then died an often painful death in AIDS, wasn't fun! And it got very boosted because of the media's scaremongering propaganda. The newspapers didn't care if what they published was true or not, only that it sold. They did everything to scare people, everything to keep alive the fear of the public in order to make as much money as possible for as long as possible. And now we are there again! When they describe today's "plague" as the most dangerous in human history, so dangerous that the whole world must be

vaccinated, they are lying to us straight to the face! They also lie when they claim that no healthcare professional has ever experienced anything like this before. But this is what reality looks like in healthcare and has always looked like! People suffer from painful diseases, people are injured, and people die. We will all die sooner or later. The fact that healthcare is kneeling more than ever is due to politicians' savings and withdrawn hospital beds. This is because they invest money in various administrative services instead of in healthcare staff. This is because care has for a long time been downgraded and with that dismantled. This is why the resources in some situations are not enough, not because a "plague" has hit us.

Charles Richter
Agree. The spread of the coronavirus covid-19 gave no reasonable cause for panic or for such drastic measures that were taken almost immediately, so I soon realized that it wasn't about protecting people or building public health but about gaining global control through mass vaccination with the threat of illness and death as AIDS. And it has obviously worked.

Jacob Gergis
Effective propaganda, which aims to influence the masses, should be focused on emotion and not reason, since people mostly let emotion determine their actions. It must also consist of a few, intelligible points, which are repeated over and over until the goal is reached. If you become versatile, you destroy the effect, because people can't deal with it and become confused and indecisive. The propaganda should not

be objective and unconditionally search for the truth but only serve its own specific purpose. That's what Hitler knew and used.

Sandra and I have been friends since high school. She told me everything and I told her everything. Or almost everything anyway. She was very in love with Mats, and when she got pregnant, her happiness was complete. She had always wanted children.

Everything in the garden was lovely until Maja was about five years old. Then she told me that Mats had started to become violent. I was very surprised, because that wasn't the picture I had of him at all. But people can change. Sandra was very sad and showed me bruises she had gotten from his pushes and blows. When I asked why he had started doing it, she said that she thought he was stressed and burned out by his job and that she and Maja were too much for him. He couldn't stand anything and just wanted to be left alone, she said, and it got worse with each passing day.

Eventually she started writing a diary to have proof if she couldn't take it anymore and had to report him. She sent it to me in a file that she filled in gradually. She wanted it to be in safe keeping if he went too far and succeeded to "end" her, as she said. I tried to get her to leave him and report him to the police, but she didn't want to.

But she made him move out anyway. She agreed that he should meet Maja, although she felt hesitant, because he was still "completely out of order", as she said, and couldn't be trusted. And one day when Maja had been with him, and Sandra picked her up at the day-care centre, Maja was completely blue on her lips and could hardly walk. She said she had leg pain. When she took off her pants at home, Sandra saw that her legs were full of bruises, and when she asked what had happened, Maja didn't want to tell her. When Sandra asked if it was dad who had done it, Maja said it was so, but she refused to explain how it had happened. Sandra photographed the injuries and sent the pictures to me. She reported him to the police for child abuse in connection with her reporting him for the assault on herself in the parking garage, and then she showed the pictures of Maja's injuries to the police. Maja was interrogated, and during the interrogation it emerged that Mats had on another occasion locked her in a dark room and let her lie in there and cry herself to sleep.

But he was never convicted of child abuse because there was no clear evidence. Maja told the police that she had gotten the bruises on her legs at day-care, and that it wasn't her dad who had hurt her at all. She only said that because she was afraid of Mats, Sandra said. But he was acquitted of both the child abuse and the assault on Sandra in the garage. Sandra couldn't understand it and regretted that she hadn't presented the diary, which clearly showed what Mats had done to her before and what he was capable of. But she corrected that mistake the next time he attacked her.

– *Now you do as I say, you little brat!*
   – *I don't have to obey you, cause you're not my dad!*
   – *Just do as I say, because otherwise…*
   – *You must not hit children.*
   – *Do as I say then!*
   – *No, I just do as Mum says, cause you're not my dad!*

FRIDA

Abuse of women: It's common for the man to hit the woman in the face. She is often inflicted with injuries in the form of bruising and swelling around the eyes, nose fractures, jaw fractures, mucosal injuries in the mouth, and lip and tooth injuries. On her upper arms she gets bruises after hard grips, and on her forearms defence injuries that occur when she holds up her arms and tries to protect herself from blows. She can also get strangulation marks or burn marks and injuries from weapons, but usually the man only uses his hands when he attacks her.

When it comes to child abuse, the picture is much the same.

There is a great disorder in the room and there are blood stains on the floor and on the walls. In the bed lies a boy about five years old without a quilt or a blanket. He has vomited on the pillow and his hair is sticky. He is bleeding from his nose, and his pyjamas are bloody. Below his right eye he has a severe subcutaneous bleeding. He lies with his eyes closed and breathes weakly. His skin is pale and sweaty, and he doesn't respond when spoken to. On both backs of his hands, he has several deep burns as from a cigarette.

THE DIALOGUE

MATS: I found out that Sandra had informed the day-care centre that she had been given sole custody of Maja and that she lived under police protection and therefore couldn't leave Maja at day-care anymore. Later I also learned that she had reported me for abusing Maja. A criminal investigation was launched, and the family law centre made a report of concern. Sandra and I were called for talks, but Sandra didn't show up. After the investigation, the family law centre determined that I had taken care of Maja in the best way possible.

Later, the police announced that Maja had been taken in for questioning. The family law centre had let a person from there come along as a companion, I was told, but I hadn't been informed. When I talked to Maja afterwards, she was very affected by the incident. I didn't want to pressure her, but I understood that it had been about the same accusations as before, that I would have locked her up and abused her. I found it very unpleasant to be accused of harming my own child, whom I loved and just wanted to protect. It was hard to be accused once again of things I hadn't done. Those around me wondered, of course, what was going on, and I didn't know how to explain it. At the same time, I had submitted a lawsuit to the district court to get sole custody of Maja, so it was a very intense period at the time.

FRIDA: Sandra accused you of abusing both herself and Maja?

MATS: Yes.

FRIDA: And as proof that you had abused her, she referred to her diary?

MATS: Yes, it was word against word. I felt completely powerless.

FRIDA: Caroline, who kept the diary for Sandra, still has it and promised to send it to me.

MATS: Good. Then it will be judged by the right person.

FRIDA: Did you recognize Sandra's way of writing in the diary?

MATS: No, not at all.

FRIDA: What was wrong?

MATS: That the text was so clearly worded. She would never have been able to write like that.

FRIDA: Did you think she had been helped to write it?

MATS: Yes, either that, or she had copied other people's texts.

FACEBOOK

Lennart Lindh
We queue at the check-out counter at Ica. The lady behind me is talking very loudly on her cell phone. "Vaccine? No, I'll skip it. I've heard it can make you so sick." What do you say? What do you do?

Karolina Östberg
Cry.

Margareta Södergren
Takes a step back and stamps on her foot.

Selma Forsell
I felt nothing after my first.

Karl-Erik Lund
Neither did I. Nothing.

Eva Andersson
Without the vaccine you can die.

Ingemar Sjögren
You have to suffer a little to keep yourself and others alive. Many don't notice a bit.

Bengt Andersson
Yes, how should one act when one hears such things? It concerns me and everyone else. Don't think that vaccine is a private matter.

Amelie Bell
She won't talk for long without the vaccine.

Cecilia Malm

Give the lady a foil face mask that fits her foil hat.

Kerstin Sundgren

You sniffle as much as you can, turn to the lady and get a huge nasty cough attack that hits her right in the face.

Bodil Holmsten

I think that those who don't get vaccinated shouldn't be allowed to participate in the opening of society either. Rather, those who have refused to be vaccinated and become ill with covid should have to pay for hospital care themselves. Nursing staff have had to pay a high price for not only the pandemic but for disobedience and stiff-necked vaccine resistance. As long as they stay out of society and I don't have to pay for their care and for their use of care and the staff who worked hard and endured difficult working conditions, I ignore them. Their behaviour is disloyal, self-inflicted, and stupid.

Karin Blomgren

It's through vaccines and by continuing to follow the recommendations that we can get out of the pandemic, says Johan Carlson, Director General of FHM.

Anders Blomqvist

And you trust him? In February 2020, he said: "The corona virus won't spread in Sweden." This spring, he said the pandemic will be over by the summer. He has a salary of just over SEK 130,000 a month.

Linda Palmqvist

Yes, don't you notice how bad he is at lying? He mostly

stands and waffles and looks down at the floor.

Lennart Lindh
Unfortunately, there are also some foil hats that spread
conspiracy theories, fake news, and false myths about
the vaccine.

Linda Palmqvist
After all, it's voluntary, right? Why should those who
don't want a vaccine be mocked and hated? Why?
That I and others with me are sceptical about just THIS
substance doesn't mean that we are anti-vaxxers and foil
hats! I am sceptical because the knowledge about this
particular product is almost non-existent. No one knows
how any side effects will affect each individual in the
short or long term. This also needs to be highlighted.

Lena Urbanska
There is no pandemic! Everything is a downright
LIE! That people get sick and die is quite clear, but of
WHAT? Why are the authorities hiding that about 270
scientists and doctors have pointed out unexplained
health risks with 5G? Why are the authorities hiding
the fact that there have been lots of reports that people
have become seriously ill when new base stations 5G
smart meters have been set up near their homes? Wuhan
= the first city in the world with fully developed 5G.
Have you ever wondered why people in Wuhan at the
beginning of the "pandemic" just "dropped dead" on
the streets when no one did the same here? The
explanation is that if you put 5G on 60 GH2, all
oxygenation in the body ceases and you die on the spot.

THE DIARY

I provoke him. I constantly provoke him. It's always my fault. I shouldn't object. I should shut up. But that can also provoke him. It annoys him that I talk, and it annoys him that I am silent. It annoys him that I look at him or that I don't look at him, that I sit, lie, or stand, that I stay or try to go away. I provoke him by just being, and that's what he is going to take out of me.

It's hard to describe what he does when he abuses me. It always goes so fast. He grabs me. He pushes me in front of him and bangs my head against the wall and throws me around and hits me.

Yesterday he strangled me. Today I have black marks on my neck.

He was angry and scolded me. I wanted to leave the room to avoid hearing more, but he didn't allow it. He grabbed my arm and threw me down on the bed. He didn't hit me. He just threw me over and held me and stopped me from leaving. I closed my eyes to avoid seeing his contorted face, but he tore open my eyelids and forced me to look at him. "Look at me when I talk to you!" he hissed.

Long periods can pass without him having an outbreak. Now it's probably all right, I think. Now it will probably never happen again. I fall for it over and over again. Then he suddenly goes crazy with anger due to a trifle and starts smashing furniture and things and me.

Today he worked up his anger to insane proportions. He screamed and roared and seized me by the throat.

He got mad and hit me, so I flew through the kitchen. I ended up at the sink and fell over. I saw his feet and his legs above me. He kicked me in the back. I tried to crawl away, but he followed and grabbed my hair and pulled up my head and hit me on the mouth, so my lower lip cracked and began to bleed.

Today he locked me in a closet. When I knocked and shouted and wanted to get out, he tied me to the shelf and stuffed an old sock in my mouth.

He grabbed my arm and wanted me to listen to him. I tore myself free and ran away, and he grabbed the bowl of boiled potatoes and threw it at me, so it hit me on one ear. Then he overturned the kitchen table with the food and all the crockery.

He punched me in the face and chased me through the house. In the kitchen, he forced me into a corner and got me down on the floor. He hit and kicked me, and I tried to protect my head with my arms. The next moment I had a kitchen knife to my throat. His eyes were black and completely insane. I cried and begged. "Shut up, or I'll cut your throat," he said. Then he threw away the knife and left.

If I object, I am either subjected to long endless monologues about how wrong I am, or I have it. He kicks up a row about nothing. He can't stand to see me. He shuts me out in the garden or locks me in the bedroom. He drags me around in the house by my clothes or my hair. He tears my books and clothes apart. He holds me by my hair and bangs his forehead against mine. He pushes, kicks, and hits me. Sometimes he says he loves me.

MATS: It was Sandra and not me who was responsible for the outbursts of anger and abuse. In the beginning, when her behaviour made me disappointed and sad, I wasn't able to just try to stop her and defend myself. Then it happened a couple of times that I, in my powerlessness and despair, fought back when she attacked me physically. Not that she was seriously hurt, but I know I lost control a few times and hit her. Sometimes I tried to bring her to reason and make her understand that she overreacted when she got angry over trifles, but I never succeeded. Her reaction was always justified, it was always me who had done wrong, and it was always she who was right. It didn't matter what I said. When she got angry, she was completely emotionally driven and couldn't be reached with words.

FRIDA: What was it that triggered her anger?

MATS: It could be anything. That I had moved an object that she had placed in a certain place, that I used the wrong towel, that I forgot things she had said. If I tried to explain how I had thought, and held on to my standpoint, it became too much for her and she was filled with an uncontrolled anger. It got even worse if I rejected her and didn't want to discuss the matter when she was irrational and just roared and screamed. Or that I refused to "explain" and answer unreasonable questions, or that I refused to give her the right when she was wrong, or that I refused to "confess" and ask for forgiveness when she demanded it, or that I objected, or that I was silent, or that I tried to leave the room to avoid participating in her outburst. She could go on for hours accusing me of what she felt I had done wrong and trying to force me to "confess" and ask for forgiveness, and when she didn't get me where she wanted with words, she resorted to physical methods. She locked me in, and she locked me out, she took away my phone, my computer, and my keys, she broke and threw away my things, she pushed me, hit me, spat on me, kicked, and screamed. Occasionally there was food and crushed crockery or broken flowerpots and soil all over the floor. In the beginning, I helped her clean up afterwards, because I couldn't stand to see the misery, but I stopped with it the same time as I stopped trying to understand and explain to myself why she did as she did. But it took years before I gave up hope that she would stop losing control and I could accept that I couldn't trust her, no matter how "normal" she behaved during the breaks. I got tired and indifferent and thought she was pitiful and pathetic when she attacked me. I stopped defending myself and let her talk or hit until she got tired. I felt completely unmoved afterwards, as if it hadn't happened at all, and I felt that what she was doing didn't have the least to do with me. Everything she did, she did to herself. I didn't participate emotionally in it anymore, and therefore it fell back on her herself. She hit me so she was injured and got bruises herself, she threw and broke things so she got extra work to clean up, she spent hours arguing so she didn't have time to do what she really had intended to do, she regretted and felt bad afterwards so she couldn't sleep. But she always regretted only for her own sake and never for what she had done to me. She never asked me for forgiveness and was always convinced that it was my fault that she had lost control. But the fact that a person's behaviour irritates you to insanity gives you neither a legal nor a moral right to resort to violence. Of course, she knew that, but it had no effect on her behaviour whatsoever.

FRIDA: So, you mean that the bruises she showed to others and claimed that you had inflicted on her were bruises that she inflicted on herself? Which she got when she hit *you*?

MATS: Yes, that's how it was. Or as it was in the beginning, when I grabbed her and held her to stop her from hitting me. Part of what she writes in the diary that I did to her was in fact what she did to me.

FRIDA: Oh my God.

MATS: Yes, but that didn't stop her from referring to the diary as evidence at the second trial.

FRIDA

He has explanations for everything I get to know, and I have to believe him, even though it seems so strange with Sandra's behaviour and all her accusations and lies. Why did she act that way? What did she think she would gain from it?

Everything she claims in the diary that Mats did to her is described in a factual and emotionless way. She describes almost no injuries, no pain, no fear, no despair, no shame. Is that credible?

Yes, it is. That was often how the women I interviewed for my book recounted their experiences. Just what concretely had happened, not how it felt.

According to Mats, it was Sandra who was aggressive towards him and not the other way around. I believe him when he says that. His attitude towards her agrees with the kind of person I think he is, and considering his way of telling me, he couldn't possibly have made it all up.

Sandra's notes are not about herself. She must have copied parts of other women's stories from books or from the Internet. I have no doubt that the experiences are authentic, but it isn't Sandra who has been abused. According to Mats, she couldn't have written in that way purely linguistically either. And there are a few details that reveal her. "He chased me through the house", "he drags me around in the house" and "he shuts me out in the garden", she writes. But she and Mats lived in an apartment and not in a house with a garden, so it couldn't possibly have happened as she describes it. And the notes are undated so that it isn't possible to determine exactly when each event occurred. Mats couldn't prove that he might not have been home on a certain day or evening, even though he had witnesses to it, as there are no time indications. Of course, she did it on purpose so as not to be exposed. But she was missing the details about the house and the garden, which proved that at least some of what she wrote in the diary wasn't about her and Mats, but about some completely different people.

Mats and I meet in the park or at open-air cafes. If we go to a café, we try to find a table for ourselves so that the recording will be as free from interference as possible. It has worked well so far, and much of what he has told me I can use in the book. Of course, my own talk doesn't belong there. I have quite a lot of material to work with now, but I still haven't decided in what form I will present it, and it feels a little frustrating. But it will sort itself out, I guess.

FINN ENGWALL

At that time, Mats worked as a doctor in the psychiatric emergency room, and I was employed there as a nurse. We had good contact, and in my opinion, he was a completely normal person with a stable psyche, a strongly developed legal consciousness and a great respect for life and all living things. I never noticed any deviations or peculiarities in him or any tendencies of violence in his disposition.

But after the separation from Sandra, he didn't feel well. He seemed tired and listless, and when I asked him what was bothering him, he told me that Sandra had started calling him at all times of the day and sending him a steady stream of text messages and e-mails. Some of the messages he got were threatening. When I asked in what way, he didn't want to go into it further. But there was a constant flow, he said. He tried to limit his answers primarily to e-mails, secondarily to text messages and ultimately to phone calls. Even though he didn't answer, he felt that he needed to read all the messages to find out what happened to Maja. He checked the phone almost around the clock and slept less than he used to and felt generally affected by the situation.

And at work, something happened that probably also affected him negatively. One night when I was standing in the reception of the emergency room, a guy who seemed a little shady came in. I asked what he wanted but got no sensible answer. Finally, he said he wanted to see the same doctor he had seen a few days before. Since he didn't know the doctor's name, I asked him to return the next day for help finding out who it might be. He then went out, but after a few minutes he came back and said he wanted to see any doctor. I registered him and asked why he applied but got no sensible answer.

Then it turned out that Mats, who was on duty, recognized him. It was decided that I and Mats would take the guy into a visiting room. As it didn't feel quite well, we asked a guard who was in the local to stay. The guy went into the room and sat with his back to the door. Mats sat opposite him and asked how he was doing. I myself stood at the door waiting. I half-listened to their conversation and heard that Mats apologized if he had the time before behaved in a way that could have been perceived as nonchalant. He then asked various questions but got only short answers. The guy sat most of the time and looked down at the floor. Mats asked if he had intended to harm himself or others. The guy then said that he had considered doing a stupid thing but that he no longer wanted to. Mats asked if it had been directed at the guy himself or at him. "At you," replied the guy. Mats then asked if he was feeling very bad, and if he wanted to see another doctor or if he wanted to go home. The guy said he wanted to go home. Both got up and Mats first left the visiting room. The guard stood outside by the lock. I myself had turned around to lock the door to the visiting room when I suddenly heard Mats screaming "knife". I turned around and saw that the guy had a knife inside his jacket. I perceived that he got the knife out of his pocket and held it in front of him at chest height. He held the knife by the handle as if to cut. Mats tried to clutch his wrist to control the knife. The guy then tried to withdraw his hand and struggled to keep the knife. He didn't want to drop it voluntarily. I don't know how it came out of his hand. It came flying and I got it away with my foot. The guy was difficult to get down on the floor, but after a good moment of wrestling match he lay there, overpowered by the guard and me.

When the emergency situation had calmed down, I stood next to a colleague and talked to the guy. During the conversation, he lay on the floor. He was handcuffed and police were on site. He was calm and orderly and no longer affected. He told us that he had been to the psychiatric emergency room earlier that week and left angry. He was dissatisfied with the doctor's way of receiving him. Then he had walked around outside. He had decided to take his own life and take the doctor, who was Mats, with him at the same time. After pondering a bit, he had decided to injure or kill the doctor but not himself. Before today's visit, he had therefore brought a knife with him. He had hoped to see the same doctor as before. He said he would have hurt the doctor if a guard and an extra male nurse hadn't been there. At the end of the conversation, he changed his mind and said that he had intended to give up the knife. He wouldn't have stabbed Mats even if he had been alone with him in the room. He had empathy for other people and wasn't capable of hurting others, he said.

I don't really know to what extent that incident affected Mats. On top of the worries about Sandra and her harassment, I think it became a little too much for him. We were used to outbursts of anger and verbal threats at work, but threats and attacks with life-threatening weapons didn't occur very often. But if a person is desperate enough or under the influence of drugs, he can do pretty much anything in my experience. You must be prepared for it all the time. And Mats continued working as usual, perhaps thinking that Sandra would eventually calm down. But there he was wrong.

When we open the door to the bedroom, the woman takes a run and throws herself with a shrill scream straight against the window. She holds up her arms to protect her face, and when the window shatters, the pieces of glass hurt her forearms and elbows. She remains standing in the shards of glass on the floor, looking defiantly at us as she takes blood from her arms and slowly begins to smear it on her face, in her hair, and on her clothes.

THE GROUP

Anders Blomqvist

FHM:

"Vaccines are carefully tested before they are made available to the public."

"The covid-19 vaccines were developed rapidly and at the same time according to the highest possible safety standards."

"The vaccines that are approved for covid-19 effectively protect against serious illness. After a vaccination, the body's immune system builds up protection against covid-19. It isn't certain that everyone who is vaccinated will receive comprehensive protection, but if you become ill, you will most likely get a milder form of the disease."

"We know that the vaccines that are approved in Sweden against covid-19 are effective and have an effect for a long time. Studies are underway to find out how long the protection after covid-19 vaccine lasts, and if a refill dose will be needed, and if so, when it should be given."

My comment:

There are no approved covid-19 vaccines today. The clinical trials won't be completed until 2022–2023 and it's only then that a decision on formal approval can be made. Despite this, Swedish authorities use the word "approved" in their information texts and call the preparations "safe" and "effective". And I hope you know that the public health authority is partly financed by the pharmaceutical industry.

Elisa Boström

What if everyone were aware of this! But I know lots of people who naively take the shots in the belief that they are the usual traditional vaccines that are carefully tested and tried for several years and not just for seven months. Even health-care professionals think that's the way it is. So the lies have been very successful in getting people to take these experimental injections or whatever you want to call them. Many even rejoice when they have become lab rats and guinea pigs for Big Pharma. It's awful!

Sara Neumann
Nobel laureate and world-leading virologist Luc Montagnier says there is no chance of survival for people who have received any form of covid-19 vaccine. There is no hope and no possible treatment for those who have already been vaccinated, he says. ("There is no hope and no possible treatment for those who have been vaccinated. We must be prepared to incinerate the bodies.")

Ilona Törnkvist
And those who haven't already died will die after their third or fourth vaxx shot.

Andrea Westergren
Wondering if they will ever start reporting on the actual number of deaths from side effects from the injections.

Ilona Törnkvist
Unfortunately, it will be kept in secret.

Malin Josefsson
New research shows that the spike protein in the covid-19 vaccines enters the bloodstream and that this is probably

what explains the reported side effects such as myocarditis and blood clots. It has also been shown that spike protein accumulates in the body's organs and can lead to future damage.

Mikael Hoover
There is no evidence whatsoever for what you are claiming. The immune system makes sure that the body gets rid of it. It doesn't stay and give effects in the body.

Nina Kaski
Unambiguous Science: "Spike protein from vaccines is harmless. The spike protein created by the vaccines isn't the same as the spike proteins on SARS-CoV-2. It has been modified to be harmless. In addition, it remains attached to the surface of the cells that produce the protein after vaccination, and doesn't travel to any other organ in your body such as your lungs or heart etc."

Mikael Hoover
Exactly. No deaths in Sweden have been proven to be due to the vaccine. And no excess mortality after vaccination has been found. What Malin is saying is wrong, misleading, and dangerous. Please stop with that and inform yourself instead.

Malin Josefsson
It isn't possible to know anything about the long-term effects until a sufficiently long time has elapsed, and it hasn't yet.

Tommy Hult
KI has been researching viruses and mRNA vaccines since

1994. There were also prototypes for corona vaccines ready 10 years ago. There was thus solid basic research collected and done even then for previous outbreaks of the corona virus. However, they weren't launched on the market because the virus variants diminished in force and the companies assessed that there was a lack of demand for the vaccines. Now with covid-19, they simply took out what they already had 10 years ago and updated it according to the specific characteristics of the new coronavirus. And updating the corona vaccines you already had (even if they weren't commercially launched), of course, went much faster than if you had to start from scratch. That's why it could go so fast.

Mikael Hoover
Exactly. We have totally forgotten that SARS (and MERS for that matter, with a significantly higher mortality rate) were once on the agenda. But the researchers haven't forgotten because they have always been aware of the situation.

Tommy Hult
3.4 percent of those affected by the coronavirus die from it, according to the World Health Organization WHO. This is more than during a normal seasonal flu, but at the same time less than what applies to other coronaviruses, such as MERS and SARS, where the mortality rate is 34 and 10 percent, respectively. Just over 96 percent of those affected by corona recover.

Andrea Westberg
Why was the new vaccine only emergency approved if it was so thoroughly researched? Well, that was because it is a com-

pletely new type of vaccine, a completely new technology, which has never been tested on humans on a larger scale before. But it's done now, so I suppose everything is fine. There are willing guinea pigs so there will be enough and more.

Malin Josefsson
There is a complete great fraud going on. We are fed with one lie after another without end. Soon it will be about coercion when trying to force people to get vaccinated. It's a nightmare. And the population allows itself to be dragged along, as no correct information about the risks is provided. Everyone who tries is systematically silenced. How many will be vaccinated before the greatest medical scandal of all time, as well as the greatest crime of all time against humanity, becomes apparent to everyone?

Philip Gardner
"A lie doesn't become truth, wrong doesn't become right, and evil doesn't become good just because it is accepted by the majority." (Booker T. Washington)

A woman had called and said that her ex threatened to shoot their joint daughter and herself if she didn't withdraw her claim for sole custody of the daughter. We went to the address because the on-duty preliminary investigation leader had got information that there could be abuse of children there. We have an obligation to go and check if the suspicion is correct when alarms about crimes against children are received.

I became involved in the matter because at the time I had an investigation regarding harassment in which the man in question was the plaintiff. When I realized that it was about the same people, and I by that had some background information, I followed the police officers who responded to the alarm. Since I am a civilian investigator, I was dressed in civilian clothes and didn't carry a weapon, but the officers were in uniform, and all three of us wore safety vests.

On the way there, the police officers asked for criminal background of the man, which showed that he hadn't been convicted of any crimes, and that he didn't have a firearms permit. The complainant was also checked, and it was then revealed that there were suspicions against her about false alarms and false imputation. We therefore informed the management centre that we could wait with the task force and negotiator.

When we rang the doorbell, a half-asleep man opened. He asked why we were there and what had happened. I don't remember how the conversation went, more than that we informed him why we were there. We were standing in the hall, and as I remember it, there was a kitchen on the left and a bedroom on the right. I opened the door to the bedroom where a child was sleeping.

I don't know how the man reacted to our arrival, but I thought he seemed tired and dejected. He explained the background and said it wasn't the first time he had been reported by his ex. He was eloquent and clear. The external commander took information for a report of false imputation and then we left. We were on site for a maximum of ten minutes. We checked the information against the report, but we didn't hold an interrogation. It was very quiet at the place when we left. We had no concern that there would have been substance in the report. The man didn't appear to be affected, and there wasn't anything to indicate an existing substance abuse problem or the like.

– *I saw your old man in town last night.*
    – *I don't think so.*
    – *What do you mean don't think so?*
    – *He doesn't live here.*
    – *Your fucking stepfather then.*
    – *And?*
    – *Don't you want to know what he did?*
    – *No, I don't.*
    – *Then you will know it anyway: He was vomiting in a litter-bin.*
    – *And?*
    – *He's a boozer, isn't he?*
    – *Yes, there you see your predestination.*
    – *What?*

THE DIALOGUE

MATS: Maja had stayed with me for three days and would stay two more days. We had had a good time, but she longed for Sandra and asked if she could call her. I helped her make the call. I only talked to Sandra for a few minutes, and I said nothing disturbing. Maja and I sat in the living room, and she talked to Sandra herself. After a while, she handed me the phone and left. Sandra told me that the prosecutor had decided that the police would come and pick Maja up at my place. I couldn't bear to discuss the matter with her and ended the call. Then I went after Maja. She was sad and told me that Sandra had said that I wasn't her real dad and that she would be taken from me. I explained that it wasn't true and that she didn't have to worry.

At night I was awakened by the doorbell. When I opened the door, two policemen and one policewoman stood outside and asked to enter. I wondered what had happened, and one of the policemen told me that an alarm had been received about an ongoing crime where I threatened to shoot my daughter. I understood at once that it was Sandra who had called. I didn't have a licence to carry a gun and didn't own a weapon, so there was no reason for her to believe that I had access to one. It seemed completely incomprehensible that she had presented it that way.

The police wanted to see what it looked like in the flat and how Maja was. One went into the kitchen, and one looked into the bedroom where Maja was sleeping. She woke up and saw the policemen. Afterwards, I talked to her about why the police had come and said that she had no need to be afraid.

Later I found out what Sandra had said in her call to the

police. She claimed that she had been awakened in the middle of the night by me calling and threatening her. At first, she didn't understand what I was saying because I was so drunk that I slurred and she herself was dazed with sleep. I started by talking about her having reported me for assault, then I exploded and had an outburst of rage. The last thing I said was that I would come and shoot both her and Maja. She was terrified and called 112. She couldn't describe the conversation word for word because the threats had been going on for a long time and she couldn't keep the events separate. She had received threatening calls from me on several other occasions and felt that she had no choice now but to call 112. The threats had been going on since Maja was born, when I, according to her, had begun to change my personality.

– Now you have to explain what the hell you are doing!
  – It's nothing.
  – Yes, it is! You have changed your whole fucking personality! You should seek medical attention!

FRIDA: Oh my God. She can't have been quite right in the head to behave like that?

MATS: No, probably not. But because I was in a close relationship with her, and her behaviour was directed at me personally, I found it very difficult to consider her as a patient.

FRIDA: Yes, I understand that.

MATS: It wasn't her doctor I wanted to be but her…

FRIDA: Mm.

…

FRIDA: How do you see the psychiatric profession?

MATS: Well, what should I say… My first thought is that it's difficult to exercise it satisfactorily.

FRIDA: Why?

MATS: In my opinion, neither the conversation nor the treatment situation in a psychiatric clinic is designed to promote real communication between doctor and patient. During my clinical years, I realized that many of my colleagues weren't only poor at communication but were even totally uninterested in what their patients had to say. Hospital routines and psychiatric treatment are basically inhibitory rather than emotionally beneficial. The patient is expected to talk honestly about his feelings, but if he tries to comment on what he thinks is going on, he is often dismissed as confused and crazy. But the language of the so-called lunatic is a unique phenomenon that you can learn to understand and respond to. Instead of trying to force the patient to express himself rationally and "comprehensibly", you should look beyond the possible diagnosis and listen openly and unconditionally to his statements.

FRIDA: Can't you do that then?

MATS: Yes, within certain limits. As a psychiatrist, you must try to observe the patient based on his or her social and experiential reference points and not judge in advance strange behaviour as illness. During the patient's attempt to communicate with those around him, it isn't the psychiatrist's task to moralize about the right or wrong in the person's world of experience. The doctor must instead be familiar with many patterns of communication, both to be able to talk to the patient and to be able to listen, no matter how peculiar the patient's language is. What's experienced by the person who is described as insane isn't really incomprehensible. It simply occurs in another dimension of reality, much like in a waking dream.

FRIDA: Mm.

– *How are you?*
 – *I don't know.*
 – *What thoughts do you have?*
 – *No special ones.*
 – *What do you feel then?*
 – *Nothing special.*

He sounds tired and uncommitted, and I feel like I can't make myself understood. There are no words for what's going on inside me. I register what's happening and understand that it's wrong, but I can't explain it because I don't know what it is.

MATS: What's usually called mental illness is in my opinion not an illness but an expression of emotional suffering. Often a person who has been diagnosed as mentally ill is the emotional scapegoat for disorders in a family or at work and can in fact be the healthiest member of the group. The symptoms can manifest themselves slowly or quickly, quietly or explosively, immediately or after a long time and are often started with the help and encouragement of the patient's next of kin.

FRIDA: Mm. What do you do if the patient's condition is caused by a traumatic event then?

MATS: When to help a person who has been through difficult and shocking experiences that she doesn't have the strength to take in emotionally, you must not rush her. Denial is a way of "resting" from a reality that feels too difficult to bear, and you must not deprive a person of her denial. But in the long run, the price of rest is high. Denial costs a lot of energy and prevents you from grieving over your changed life situation. Denial is a deadlock while grief is a process that leads to liberation.

FRIDA: What should a good doctor do to help then?

MATS: In the first place, just listen. When you feel lonely, confused, and scared, you hope that another person will see how you feel and be present, show interest and, if possible, provide security and care. There is a risk that you as a doctor become too passive and leave too much to a patient who can't cope with it. Or you can become too active and push too much before the patient is ready. In other words, you can damage the relationship by being so withdrawn that the patient doesn't grasp who you are, or by being so compelling that the patient doesn't have the strength to keep up. It's a balancing act. But listening openly and unconditionally is the main thing and is what's often not done. Sometimes it's the diagnosis itself that gets in the way. Decisive for how the collection of clinical signs and symptoms that determine whether it's about psychosis, neurosis, psychopathy, an organic brain injury or something else, is who conducts the examination and where it takes place – at home, in a hospital, at a police station, on a street or other – and the patient's insight into his situation.

FRIDA: Mm.

I have asked him to stop, but he doesn't stop. Finally, I put on my jacket and go out. I take nothing with me. It's dark and rainy outside. Cars glide past on the street. I float and disappear. Nobody knows where I am. I am lost and can't find my way back.

- *Why are you sitting here?*
    - *I'm resting.*
    - *But you will get soaking wet.*
    - *It doesn't matter.*
    - *Do you live nearby?*
    - *Yes, not far.*
    - *Not far? Then I think you should go home now.*
    - *No, it's too cramped there, and then I get dangerous.*

FRIDA: When Sandra died, did you work at the psychiatric emergency room?

MATS: Yes, that's right.

FRIDA: One of your colleagues from that time has told me that you felt pretty bad the time before.

MATS: Yes, that's right. Is it Finn you have talked to?

FRIDA: Yes. But you kept on working?

MATS: Yes.

FRIDA: He also told me about an incident with a man armed with a knife who came to the reception.

MATS: Yes, I remember that. There was a trial as well.

FRIDA: How did you experience the attack?

MATS: It was unpleasant of course. But it left no deeper traces, I think.

FRIDA: How did it end? At trial, I mean.

MATS: The crime he was convicted of was attempted aggravated assault. The minimum sentence for that crime, if completed, was at that time a year in prison, I think. But since it was only an attempt, and he also had a mental disorder that made him impaired in his ability to control his actions, the sentence was six months. But he killed himself before it was executed.

FRIDA: Oh, he did.

MATS: Yes. There are so many who feel bad and aren't able to live, and there is so little healthcare can do to help. Lonely people lie dead in their flats without being noticed by those around them until much later. Maybe not until the smell reveals what has happened.

FRIDA: Yes, I know. You read about it sometimes. I have read about it.

He is lying on his stomach in the hall with the left half of his face flattened against the floor. The body is in a state of dissolution with fluid formation and greenish discoloration of the skin. Beneath the body, a dark, glistening pool has spread. There is no visible damage to the body. The stench in the flat due to the putrefaction and the liquid that has formed is terrible.

FRIDA

In my medical record it says that I am sad and feel bad. I don't want to be admitted to the hospital, but I am persuaded by my brother and a doctor. During the admission interview, I seem unjustifiably suspicious, reticent, and negative. I deny hallucinations, but it can't be ruled out that I am hallucinating even though I don't admit it. In the ward, I keep to myself and don't make contact with carers or fellow patients. I am suspicious, introverted, and inaccessible and show weak signs of unjustified aggression. After two weeks, I request to be discharged. They try to persuade me to stay with the motivation that I, with the symptom picture I have, will find it difficult to manage outside. I don't realize myself how bad I am. But lack of insight into the disease, and other symptoms that I have shown in the ward, are not enough to write a care certificate that would enable a forced admission.

I have lost my foothold and am floating as in an empty space. It scares me. I don't know what will happen or how long it will last. I understand that I am alone and have gotten lost, and I am afraid I will never find my way back. I feel so weak, and the road ahead seems so long. Will I be able to continue to fight against all the difficulties that overwhelm me? Isn't it better to just give up?

FACEBOOK

Sverker Jansson
Today when I was listening to the radio, the channel changed completely by itself. Last time it happened, I thought it was due to atmospheric disturbances, but now antivaxxers have made me understand that it's 5G, which I got with the first vaccine injection, that is the cause. Today I will take the second jab. Wondering if I'll have access to Radio Luxembourg afterwards?

Allan Skoog
Ha ha, fun!

Magdalena Burling
You also become magnetic. Metals will be attracted to you and stick to your body.

Daniela Ståhl
Yes, the state wants to microchip us with vaccines. Bill Gates wants to kill half the world's population.

Peter Ehnmark
After the second shot, you don't need a radio. You get all the channels just by turning your body.

Fredrik Öberg
Good there, Sverker! I'm really happy to see how people continue to get vaccinated. How the statistics tick, how we move towards a fully vaccinated society.

Georg Smedberg
You are not funky then? For the second dose, I mean. You got pretty sick after the first one, didn't you? Had to

go to the emergency room and everything, if I remember it correctly? Right?

Astrid Nyström
The second dose has fewer side effects than the first one. Personally, I didn't get any side effects at all.

Georg Smedberg
Or vice versa. I read about a guy who died from the second. He became short of breath from the first and died from the second.

Astrid Nyström
It only happens one in a million.

Georg Smedberg
Well, I don't know. In any case, personally I wouldn't dare to take the risk. I'm not one of those antivaxxers that you for some reason feel the need to deride, but I don't trust this particular vaccine.

Sanna Olberg
Yes, show those of us who choose not to take this vaccine some consideration and respect. Don't call us crazy and disloyal. You don't know a shit about how it will go! It may be you who take these experimental injections that will ultimately burden the healthcare system. Who can be sure of anything in these times? Don't call us cowards because we are not. We have been open to ALL information and have dared to listen even to what's difficult, uncomfortable, and unpleasant. Don't try to persuade us to "roll up" when we have decided to assert the right to decide over our bodies.

Ove Jansson
Go to sleep.

Marika Strandberg
I didn't feel a bit after my second. Don't listen to the prophets of woe, Sverker! Listen and trust science! At least I do.

Gunilla Gelin
I say only one thing: DON'T TOUCH OUR CHILDREN! They should not be exposed to this "vaccine" or dangerous PCR tests or ineffective face masks! Let them live and breathe freely and build up their natural immune system!

Stella Lovén
Vaccination of children is already planned. On our National Day, three professors published an article in SvD and called for vaccination of children, that is, to turn our children into guinea pigs. It's illegal and goes against a number of conventions on medical experiments. Children have a 99.997 percent chance of surviving covid and yet they should be vaccinated!

Gunilla Gelin
Over my dead body!

Betty Keeler
Yes, it's totally sick!

Stella Lovén
You should definitely not vaccinate your children against covid-19. Vaccines should not be given unless there is a relatively high risk of serious illness, disability, or death

from a disease. Children run an extremely low risk of becoming seriously ill with covid-19. According to statistics from the USA, common flu is much more serious for children. Children are not vaccinated against the flu, so why should they be vaccinated against covid? We know far too little about the side effects of the vaccines both in the short and long term, so giving experimental preparations to children is both unethical and dangerous.

Astrid Nyström
Why do you think you know better than the professionals in the Public Health Agency and others who recommend vaccines to 12-year-olds? Unbelievable...

Lennart Lindh
Too bad for the children who want it but have foil hats for parents.

Pontus Hägg
The idea is that the spread of infection ceases if a sufficiently large part of the population is vaccinated or immune. Therefore, children and young people must also be vaccinated so that fewer people can be infected with the virus and spread it further.

Jonas Malmberg
It really must be a lousy vaccine if children, who almost never get sick from covid, need to be vaccinated to protect already vaccinated adults.

Inga-Britt Lovén
So good that we can finally stop this plague.

Markus Haglund
Yes, stopping the spread of infection is the only way to end the pandemic.

Ove Jansson
Hope they lower to six-year-olds eventually, so everyone who goes to school can be vaccinated.

Gabriel Alm
Vaccination protects against both infection and the spread of infection, but not one hundred percent. It's the unvaccinated who will spread the infection among themselves now.

Conny Berg
Yeah, it's spreading, said he who crapped in the fan.

Jonas Malmberg
No, it's not, Gabriel. Even vaccinated people can become infected and pass on the infection. The vaccine thus doesn't protect against the spread of infection, only against serious illness and death. But a strong and natural immune system protects better and longer (sometimes for life) than a vaccination does. Those who are vaccinated will have to take updated doses as the effect diminishes or the virus mutates, which it can do in principle as many times as you like. The disadvantage is that repeated vaccinations become an accumulated burden on the natural immune system.

Lennart Lindh
You are talking like you are stupid for real.

Petra Risberg

There are always many messages to consider, but you have to trust the expertise. Have had covid, received the first vaccine dose and am waiting for the next one. For what's the alternative, as well? You have to do what you can to end the misery!

Rose-Marie Nilsson

I believe in research and science, I believe we need vaccines to protect ourselves and others. I believe in a human view where we protect each other. I call for more openness, tolerance, and nuanced discussions about this, which has become so difficult to talk about calmly and objectively in most contexts. Light and love to us all!

TINA TAYLOR

When Mats reported Sandra to the police for harassment and false accusations, I understood that it was a countermove on his part to avoid admitting that he was guilty of everything she had accused him of and a way to get sole custody of Maja. When she told me about the incident in the garage and showed me the bruise on her arm and the bump on her head and went to the health centre to have the injuries documented, I knew she wasn't lying. He had abused her for a long time, she said, but she had never reported him to the police before. There was also a diary, where she had written about it, but I didn't know then. It came out at the trial. But no one believed what she said. She had made up a lot of acts of violence that Mats would have committed against her just to be able to put him there, it was alleged. She had harassed him and lied about almost everything, and it could be proved. Or not be proved, but she wasn't credible, it was considered. She was sentenced to pay twenty thousand in damages to him, although it was he who had harassed and abused *her*. It must have annoyed her exceedingly that it turned out that way. I remember thinking that. With my knowledge of her, I think that's how she reacted. She didn't want to give up. She never wanted to give up when she knew she was right and it didn't turn out the way she wanted. For example, I remember once when Mats had recently moved away from her, and she and I were out at a restaurant together, how mad she became when a guy rejected her. It started with her approaching him and sitting on his lap, and then she wanted to dance. But he rejected her because she was drunk. When he later danced with another girl, she walked up to them and pressed herself in between them and kind of took him over. The guy had to ask his friends to free him. In a sober state she was happy and pleasant, but when she had been drinking, she became intrusive and could approach any unknown guy and behave inviting. By acting that way, she exposed herself to risks. It didn't help that I warned her. Once she was close to being raped. Or if she actually was. It was at a party, and she was drunk and provocative, so it was no wonder that it happened. It was before she met Mats. There were three guys, I think, and all three pulled a train on her in the bedroom while the rest of the company partied on in the room next door. That time she also called me afterwards. At first, she was angry with herself because she had been drinking too much and attracted them, as she said, but then her story began to tend to rape. When I think back, that was often how she did, that she changed reality a bit, so that it would suit her better and give her what she wanted. But that Mats abused her and threatened to kill her was definitely not made up. He did it too, in the end. Killed her, that is.

She lies naked in bed with her legs apart. Her breasts, which are large and heavy, fall out to the sides and are stained with blood. She has injuries to her face and neck. The eyelids are partly closed and discoloured. The eyelashes have stuck together by tears or mucus. She is bloody in her hair and around her nose and mouth. On her arms and thighs, she has large dark bruises.

THE JUDGEMENT

The gun threat

From the emergency call that was played at the main hearing, it appears that Sandra Brolin initially states that Mats Wiklund had kidnapped their daughter and does not mention the threat against her in more detail. Her accusations then escalate during the conversation. The escalation happens in the district court's opinion when the police state that they will not respond due to her information since Mats Wiklund is a joint guardian with her. It is only towards the end of the emergency call that Sandra Brolin tells the police that Mats Wiklund has threatened to kill Maja Brolin and herself and that Mats Wiklund is armed and under the influence of drugs and that they should therefore take the threat seriously. All in all, the district court considers that the emergency call supports that the threat, that Sandra Brolin stated that Mats Wiklund during their conversation expressed, did not take place, but that it was a question of a reconstruction after the event and that this information was thus not truthful.

The abuse

What Mats Wiklund has stated about him not being at the scene, and that Sandra Brolin's story isn't true, is to some extent supported by the fact that the surveillance film obtained during the preliminary investigation in connection with the alleged crime, has not shown that any assault took place or that Mats Wiklund was at the scene. During the main hearing, however, Sandra Brolin stated that the assault took place in a place other than where the surveillance camera was located. It should be added that Sandra Brolin, also regarding this charge, has left a vague and incoherent story on several important points. At interrogation during the investigation, she has stated that she had a bump in her head after the incident, which she also has confirmed at the main hearing, but according to the cited records, this injury was not noticed by doctors when examining her after the incident. The doctor has only noted bruises as injuries during the examination. Sandra Brolin has stated that the doctor did not touch her head during the examination and therefore did not detect the swelling. The district court considers, in light of Sandra Brolin's informing the doctor that she had had her head banged against a concrete pillar so she had been unconscious for about an hour, that it can be considered very unlikely that the doctor at the health centre did not perform an examination of her head. The record and its lack of documented injuries to the head thus provides some support for Sandra Brolin not being inflicted with injuries to the back of the head in the manner alleged. Sandra Brolin has also repeatedly talked about a witness but has not been able to provide complete information about him during the preliminary investigation, which has resulted in him not being able to be located. At the main hearing, Sandra Brolin has stated that what is said in the interrogation is not true but that she has given the police a complete registration number. In view of the fact that it concerns notes from police interrogations, the district court finds that the claim that she provided a complete registration number but that the police incorrectly stated that she did not do so must be considered so improbable that it should be assessed as a reconstruction after the event. So even in this part, her story thus contains contradictory and illogical information.

THE DIALOGUE

FRIDA: I have read the judgement and know that you were acquitted.

MATS: Yes, the prosecutor cancelled all ongoing criminal investigations, and I was able to prove to my employer that I was innocent. It was a great relief.

FRIDA: Yes, I understand that.

MATS: I had to counter-report her to try to get exculpated. Otherwise, I wouldn't have had a chance to get sole custody of Maja. If it had only been about myself, I might not have cared about it, but now it was about Maja as well. But the custody investigation was never finished.

FRIDA: Why were you so indulgent with Sandra? Or lenient is perhaps a better word.

MATS: I have always been the one who listens and sets myself aside, both in my job and privately. It was difficult for me to leave that role.

FRIDA: Mm.

MATS: Actually, I have never thought about what a lonely position this is. I'm just used to not advertising myself.

FRIDA: Yes, it happens easily.

MATS: This about always being the "expert" who is expected to understand and help... As if I would never need understanding or help myself... It affects your self-concept and behaviour to never give yourself the opportunity to show yourself weak and needy. You put yourself aside, and that makes it difficult for other people to reach you. And you get the feeling that other's needs are always greater than yours. You don't know anyone you can trust and want to turn to for help. You don't think you even need it. I have been so in the role and habit of being there for others that I have never bothered to question it. And the conviction that no one can cope with me or be interested runs deep. Privately, I haven't surrounded myself with strong, competent people. All of this is perhaps actually a protection against the fear of emotional closeness and reciprocity.

FRIDA: How do you feel now then?

MATS: That I want to break that habit and try to show more of myself.

FRIDA

I am not telling Mats anything. It's just me who knows how similar we are and how alike we have acted. He sometimes asks, but I dare not trust him.

How will he reach me? How do I reach him? What could make me feel engaged again? I am committed to this with the book, but not deeply and emotionally. It's just a job. Other people don't concern me, and no one interests me. Not Mats either, although I know quite a lot about him now and think I understand him. Why don't I feel closer to him than I do?

He doesn't trust me. He doesn't want to tell me the whole truth. Or is it me who isn't open enough to *him*? Because I am not. When he talked about how he has always put himself aside, and how he had lenience with Sandra, I could have told him about Fabian. But I didn't.

He was so dissatisfied with everything. He came home and vented his anger and frustration over everything he thought was wrong and had no idea how it felt to me. If he had cared about me, he wouldn't have been able to do so. He thought only of himself. I also just thought of him and believed I was helping him by listening to him, but actually I just let myself be taken advantage of.

And it didn't help. It never ended. I tried to tell him sometimes, that I didn't want to hear it, and that I was tired of him always complaining, and then he said: "Tell me to shut up then!" But if I did, he got angry and said I was incomprehensible and didn't care about him. And I didn't *want* to rebuke him, because I thought it would be his feeling for me, that he liked and respected me, that should have stopped him from doing what he did. I didn't think I would have to assert myself or try to control his behaviour.

And every time it happened, I put away my disappointment that we couldn't be two but would just devote ourselves to him all the time. Because I thought he needed it, and that it would be better when he had come out with the worst. And maybe it was, temporarily, but I couldn't understand how he could just take for granted that he had the right to *do* so to me.

And it never ended, because he was constantly dissatisfied, and I had to hear it every day. I would be ashamed, and feel as if I had committed an abuse, if I daily forced another person to listen to my dissatisfaction with how wrong others behave and how dogged by bad luck I am. And I don't understand how he, who apparently imagined that he would feel fine if only everyone else behaved and adhered to the rules, could do what he did, because he didn't take responsibility for his own behaviour and he didn't show consideration for others. Not for me anyway.

It would have felt good if I could have talked to him about myself sometimes, but there was no room for that. It was all just about him, about how difficult his life was. Why did I put up with it? I knew that he would never take his responsibility so that we became equal and got the same amount of space. He was like a child who couldn't set limits for himself if no one forced him to. Sometimes I tried, although I didn't want to, and then he said: "Do you want me to move? Do you want to get rid of me? Do you want to throw me out? Do you think that living alone would make me feel better?" That *I* perhaps would feel better living alone he didn't think of at all.

He was pathetic, and even more pathetic was I who let it

go on. I knew he didn't care about me and just took advantage of me. But it wasn't bad enough, and not painful enough, for me to end it. And I felt responsible for him and wanted to help him. But he never listened to me when I gave him advice and tried to make him understand how limiting his behaviour was and how much it hindered him in his life. It was as if his negative attitude had become a part of himself that he couldn't be without. Every time he felt down and out of control, he blamed others instead of dealing with himself. He didn't understand that it was his negative attitude that was the problem and not external circumstances or other people's behaviour. I don't know how many times I tried to explain it to him. But he refused to understand that he was responsible for his feelings and that he could choose how he wanted to react. He refused to take control of himself and change his negative attitude which made him see all people as selfish and ruthless. He couldn't see that he himself was selfish and ruthless. At least to me.

Eventually I realized I had to give up on him. If he didn't want to help himself, there was no point in me trying to do it either. I became indifferent to him and no longer cared what he said or did. He had to associate with his dissatisfaction and bitterness without me, and I was no longer affected by it. When I had dissociated from him so that I could see what he was doing from a distance and without reacting personally to it, my contempt for him increased every time it happened. In the end, he couldn't even arouse my contempt, and I wondered how long it would take until he discovered that he was alone in everything and what would happen then. How would he react when he noticed that I no longer engaged in his problems, and I clearly showed my disinterest in his expressions of dissatisfaction?

I soon found out. At first, he accused me of being "weird" and having a "changed personality". Then he claimed that I hated him and wanted to get rid of him. And when I explained how I felt, he threatened to kill me first and then himself. Didn't I understand what "fucking pressure" I was putting on him? Didn't I understand how impossible what I "demanded" was?

But I demanded nothing. It was the opposite, that I had finally given up hope of him and stopped taking responsibility for him.

THE GROUP

Joakim Waldt

On 22 June, FHM announced that vaccination of persons under the age of 18 will begin this autumn. Then the age limit will be lowered from 18 to 16 years.

Tove Lindvall

Why are they so ANXIOUS for these young people to get vaccinated? You feel in your whole being that something is WRONG!

Felicia Leander

Yes, it's so insanely sick!

Joakim Waldt

According to statistics, the mortality was lower than usual in the group 0–70 years in 2020. So far in 2021, Sweden has also had lower mortality in total. According to the Swedish Social Insurance Agency, there has been neither an increase in occupancy in the ICU nor in number of sick leaves. People between the ages of 0–19 barely exist in the ICU according to statistics. So why is it so urgent with our young people now?

Pontus Hägg

This is because they can otherwise pass the infection on to others and keep the pandemic alive.

Malin Josefsson

No, it's an ongoing clinical study, a medical experiment, a research project, which applies to a new form of technology, a gene therapy product that hasn't been proven to stop infection.

Magnus Nygren
Infection isn't equal to severe illness and death.

David Norlin
That we have lower mortality can't be true, can it? Aren't people dying with covid every day?

Hans Thorén
Yes, those who think that there is a lower mortality have probably not looked at the statistics. Or maybe they are blind. Or they are not so good at numbers. Or they don't give a shit about numbers and say what they think seems best. It's not lower but excess mortality that applies now. Anyone who claims that there is no excess mortality due to covid-19 is either extremely incompetent or a simple liar. Since the beginning of April 2020, Statistics Sweden has published preliminary weekly statistics on mortality and there it's clearly visible.

Per Eriksson
Excuse me for saying this, but it's probably you, Hans, who haven't read it properly. If you count the deaths as a percentage of the population, which of course must be done to get a true picture, there was absolutely no excess mortality in 2020.

Rolf Karlsson
Yes, that's how it is. There may have been no lower mortality, but absolutely no excess mortality in 2020.

Per Eriksson

This is how the National Board of Health and Welfare describes the reporting of deaths in covid-19: "This compilation includes those who have influenza as a contributing or underlying cause of death, as well as patients who are cared for in specialist care with an influenza diagnosis and then died within 30 days irrespective of cause of death." Again, IRRESPECTIVE of the cause of death. Of course, there will be many then.

Rolf Karlsson

Reduce the number of deaths reported by 94 % and you have a figure that probably corresponds to reality. There are only about 6 % of the deaths classified as covid cases where covid has been the only significant factor.

Jill Jonasson

The statistics don't lie. I trust the statistics.

Per Eriksson

Never before have governments changed the way deaths are reported. Before covid came, coronavirus was never recorded as the leading cause of death when a person died of heart disease, cancer, diabetes, other autoimmune diseases, or other serious diseases. Then it was the disease that was stated as the cause of death, while for example influenza or pneumonia was stated as a contributing cause. Now it's the opposite, and one may wonder why?

Salvador Scott

This is the first time in my life that I have heard public health authorities go out and say: "The vaccines are very good, but if you are vaccinated you can still get the disease. It may also be that they can't stop the spread of infection." It isn't normal! The point of a vaccine is to be protected! In what way are the vaccines "very good" if they don't protect against the disease or the spread of infection? They can also cause very serious side effects, both immediate and long term. Nevertheless, the authorities continue to tell us: "The vaccine is safe and effective, and the benefits greatly outweigh the risks, so go and get vaccinated!" Why does no one count on people's natural immune systems anymore?

Per Eriksson

I quote: "Researchers at, among others, the Washington University School of Medicine in USA have found that even a mild infection with SARS-CoV-2 results in the activation of so-called long-lived plasma cells. The researchers analysed bone marrow samples from subjects and saw that these cells are activated after a corona infection. The result (presented in the journal Nature) means that even after a mild infection, the body will produce antibodies against the coronavirus for a long time to come. The cells can live for 60 or 70 years and are part of our long-term immune system. However, the levels are low, so a person may have these antibodies although they cannot be found with a standard antibody test. Whether the vaccine also activates these immune cells, however, no one knows yet."

Håkan Nilsson
Even researchers disagree: "Previous coronavirus infection does not necessarily protect against covid-19 in the long run, say researchers at Oxford University. In the study that was done, most people who developed symptomatic disease had a measurable immune system six months later, while a quarter did not have it. More than 90 % of those with asymptomatic infection had no appreciable immune system 6 months later. The conclusion was that vaccine immunity is more reliable because people are given a standard dose in the usual way."

Per Eriksson
I don't understand the last sentence of your quote, Håkan.

Håkan Nilsson
Neither do I, Per. But that's what it says in the text.

Jonas Malmberg
Active immunization occurs when the body is exposed to an infectious agent and thus activates the immune system and begins to produce antibodies to fight it. This can happen in two ways: Either that you become infected with a virus naturally, with some risk of getting sick. Or you can get a vaccine that contains a weakened variant of the virus, and which then triggers the body to form antibodies that then survive and can protect you the next time you are exposed to the same virus. Active immunization often provides long-term, (sometimes lifelong) protection. However, it may take a while until the body has developed protection, which is why doctors recommend risk groups to, for example, get vaccinated against

the annual flu a few months before it is expected to break out. However, no vaccine provides 100 % protection.

Frans Rappe
I'm completely healthy and since I haven't taken a single vaccine since I was a child, I don't know at all how my body would react to the vaccine. In that situation, it feels completely wrong to fuck up my probably strong immune system by injecting a substance into my body and risking having side effects. I'd rather take the virus than the vaccine.

Leonard Stagge
This isn't an ordinary vaccine but a weapon, which in addition to graphene, nano, and everything else in living nanotechnology is transmitted via shedding, so what does a good immune system help against it? These substances make us controlled, give us certain emotions, and can even kill us. This is the underlying purpose of the poison injections.

The blinds are folded down and the curtains are almost completely drawn. No lamps are lit except for a floor lamp with a red screen next to the sofa. In front of the sofa is a table with overflowing ashtrays, dirty bottles and glasses, used needles, emptied capsules, tampons, coffee filters, and bloody swabs. There are blood stains on the floor, and the smell in the room is pungent and musty. The girl sitting on the sofa has a syringe in her hand. She presses her left upper arm against her chest and holds her forearm rigidly outstretched in front of her with a clenched fist. The next moment she inserts the needle into the bend of her arm, and when blood flows into the syringe, she presses by means of the plunger the cloudy mixture into her arm, quickly pulls out the needle, places her

tongue against the puncture mark, releases the syringe, falls back-
wards down on the sofa, and lies motionless with wide open eyes.

THE DIALOGUE

MATS: Yes, now you know everything about me, but I know almost nothing about you.

FRIDA: No, I don't know everything about you.

MATS: Most things.

FRIDA: Yes, maybe.

MATS: Are your parents alive?

FRIDA: No, my stepfather drank himself to death and Mum became ill and died five years ago.

MATS: That's sad to hear. Your biological father then?

FRIDA: He disappeared when I was little.

MATS: Do you have siblings?

FRIDA: Yes, a younger brother. Or half-brother, actually.

MATS: Do you meet?

FRIDA: No, not anymore. After Mum's death, he lived with me for a while, but it didn't work, and now he is in prison.

MATS: For what?

FRIDA: I don't really know. Abuse and rape, I think. We have no contact anymore. Do you have any siblings?

MATS: Yes, I also have a brother. He's a policeman.

FRIDA: Oh. Here in town?

MATS: Yes. And he knows who you are.

FRIDA: He does?

MATS: And what happened.

FRIDA: I see. Why didn't you tell me that you know?

MATS: I thought you might tell me yourself if you gained confidence in me.

FRIDA: I see.

MATS: So it wasn't just because of your book that I chose to ask you, but also because I knew you have been a police officer.

FRIDA: And what's the benefit of that, do you mean?

MATS: That you have experience of crime and criminals and are familiar with the machinery of justice. I thought it might facilitate your research.

FRIDA: Yes, it may have.

MATS: But I don't mean you have to confide in me if you don't want to.

FRIDA: No, I understand that.

MATS: Do you think I have deceived you?

FRIDA: No, I can't say that... I should have told you, I guess. But I have the same problem as you, that I have difficulty in showing myself. I'm used to listening, not talking about myself.

MATS: Yes. And besides, you don't trust me.

FRIDA: And you don't trust *me*. What's your brother's name?

MATS: Jesper Wiklund. Jeppe.

FRIDA: Yes, then I know who he is. Have you had contact with him during your time in prison?

MATS: Yes, he has visited me regularly.

FRIDA: Can I talk to him about you?

MATS: If you want to.

FRIDA: It's not that I don't believe you, but I can't just...

MATS: ...trust a murderer one-hundred-per-cent?

FRIDA: But you say it wasn't you who did it.

MATS: Yes, she was already dead when I got there.

It's moonlight and twelve degrees below zero. The hoarfrost on the walls in the underpass sparkles in the light from the streetlamp outside the entrance. The guy on the ground is motionless. Henrik shines on him with his torch and pokes at him with his foot.

– Hey there, time to pack up and find a better place to kip.

No reaction. I pull off the dirty quilt and grab his shoulder.

– If you stay here you will freeze to death.

His body is stiff, and when I examine him more closely, I discover that he is already dead.

FRIDA

He has known what happened to me when on duty all the time but hasn't told me in order to test my confidence in him. Maybe I should feel cheated, but I don't. I haven't been honest either. I haven't told him about my background, and there are questions about the murder that I don't ask him not to force him to lie, which I have a definite feeling that he would currently choose to do. I suppress my police instincts for both his and my own sake. Sooner or later, I have to stop with it if we are to be able to carry out this project. But we are not there yet.

And his brother is a police officer... I won't contact him. Meeting a colleague would mean that I exposed myself to an attention that I don't want, no matter what expression it would take. He might think that we have common experiences, and we may have, but in that case, there is nothing I would like to discuss with him. Of course, if we met, we would primarily talk about Mats, and I would get to know a little about his upbringing and original family situation, but what use would I have of that? He can tell me himself if he thinks it should be included in the book.

I am not acquainted with Jesper Wiklund, but I know who he is. He has excelled a couple of times for heroic efforts when on duty. On one occasion, he saved the life of a little boy who was close to drowning. On another occasion, he managed to stop a loaded junkie from stabbing innocent people in a shopping mall by shooting him in one leg. A good marksman, in other words. Or was he just lucky? Afterwards, he was criticized on social media for firing his weapon among a lot of people who could have been hit by the shot.

But trying to stop an aggressive person armed with a knife using only a baton is naive and doomed to fail. A knife is a life-threatening weapon that can cause devastating damage with a single stab. The murder of Sandra is clear proof of that. And personally, I have seen bloody examples of what a knife can accomplish.

Many believe that when a police officer meets a knife-wielding person who tries to attack, his education and training should enable him to wrestle down and disarm the perpetrator or at least just wound him. But a police officer who is in a threatening situation becomes as angry and afraid as any other person. At best, he is a type who through his personal qualities, his experience, and his training can handle the situation a little better than ordinary people, but definitely not as good as the superhero in an action movie, which many seem to believe.

Police officers in general want to avoid violence, and the police's accepted tactics are defensive. The national basic technology contains many useful concepts and can give police officers increased safety and security at work. The problem is that tactical models that are taught are only defensive. This means that in practice it's only possible to intervene against people who do as you say. But often you also need to be able to act offensively, especially when there is danger to life and health. But offensive methods are not regularly taught to police officers in external duty. Instead, you are forced to improvise to the best of your ability if you end up in a tense situation. You are forced to make a quick decision about the situation, environment, risks, tactics, laws, rules, emotions, obligations, and consequences. Sometimes you are forced to fire warning shots or give effective fire.

About ten meters is considered to be the smallest distance that makes it possible to get off a shot with a pistol from a holster. But then the chance of successfully placing the shot in, for example, a leg is minimal. If you add adrenaline rush, stress, and fear, you understand how difficult it is.

From the public, there is an absolute expectation that the police will act forcefully in an emergency. But why should a police officer intervene against a perpetrator and risk being prosecuted and losing his job if he fails to perform his task optimally? Why should he risk his own life to try to stop a killer who tries to attack and refuses to drop his weapon? At what point in the course of events does the public consider it justified for the police to use their service weapon? And why should a police officer make an effort to protect a public that is so quick to criticize and condemn him when he only is doing his job and constantly tries to do it in the best possible way?

Being a police officer in external duty means that you never know what to expect when you go on your shift. Being a police officer means dealing with rape, assault, robbery, murder, manslaughter, fires, riots, explosions, pub riots, domestic violence, accidents, traffic accidents, hit animals, and suicides. It means that you are threatened and hated and get all the invectives that exist at all thrown at you. It may also mean saving the life of a woman who has been brutally assaulted and nearly killed, handcuffing violent people, caring for drunk, drugged and mentally ill people, calming shocked victims and witnesses. And it means that you go on a new case immediately after reporting the previous one without first having time to eat or go to the toilet, that you continue overtime after working sixteen hours in a row and that, after being awake for more than twenty-four hours, you can't relax and sleep even though you have consumed all your energy and are exhausted to body and soul.

Being a police officer also means that you might kill another person.

FRIDA

Now Carina's boyfriend has almost killed her. She is in a coma in the intensive care unit with life-threatening head injuries. When I interviewed her for my book, he was in prison, and she said she had promised herself not to let him come back when he was released. If she managed to stick to it, maybe that's why he has attacked her now. An asshole like him can't stand being dumped.

It happened outside a restaurant she had visited together with Moa at work. Moa witnessed the assault and could identify him. First, he hit Carina with his car, so she fell over on the street, then he jumped out of the car and started kicking her in the head when she was lying on the ground. When the ambulance arrived, she was unconscious and showed only faint signs of life.

Now she is in a coma with a disfigured face and fighting for her life. Her condition is described as critical, and it's unclear if she will survive. The asshole quickly fled the scene, but he was later arrested by the police and is tied to the crime.

Carina is in an artificial coma, which means that her brain has been put out of action through total anaesthesia so that she is neither conscious nor can react to external influences. This measure is taken to allow the brain to rest and recover more easily. During an artificial coma, blood pressure, heart rate, and respiration are maintained mechanically or with the help of drugs. A person can be placed in an artificial coma using anaesthetics or by cooling. When ending the treatment, the person is taken out of the state to a normal consciousness again.

I don't want to. I don't want to be this confused and absent and empty in my head. I am ashamed. I am ashamed of how I have been, and I am ashamed of all the weird things I have done, and I am ashamed to be here. I can't stay here any longer. I have to get out of here. I have to start behaving normally and show that I am aware of reality.

THE GROUP

Jonas Malmberg

Viruses mutate, and that's completely natural. That is what viruses do to survive. And the harder a virus is fought, the more often it mutates so as not to die, one might assume. To date, the covid-19 virus has undergone four major mutations – Alpha, Beta, Gamma, and Delta. Delta will be used by the authorities to get people to keep getting vaccinated. Right now, it's claimed that two doses protect against the delta variant. When it turns out that the effect decreases even though many have taken their two doses, a third dose will be needed. It will be able to be updated with anything, and no feasibility studies or tests will be required. In the future, everyone should roll up before the annual mass vaccination, because a lot of celebrities have told us to do so, and celebrities of course know what's best for us.

Mats Öman

A well-known virologist says that mass vaccination in a pandemic is never the right way to go, because it only pushes the virus to create conditions for new, more contagious variants. And this in turn will lead to a dramatic increase in disease cases with total resistance to the injections.

Vilma Andreasson

There are already plans for more than two doses. Refill doses or so-called boosters are planned to be given this autumn, although no one knows what the effects of it will be.

Ilona Törnkvist

The third dose will be extremely fatal. Everything is fake, and now they are killing us with their medical experiments.

Casper Åhman

I quote Aftonbladet: "Despite two doses of vaccine, more and more people are getting sick with the delta variant of covid-19. This autumn, Sweden will approve updated vaccines for a third dose – and there are plans for a fourth.

"Maybe you can combine the booster dose with other vaccines, such as the flu, cold, and something new, like a cocktail", says Sweden's vaccine coordinator Roland Bergström.

Since when is there suddenly a vaccine against colds?

Vilma Andreasson

Yes, let's take the opportunity to play and experiment now that we have so many volunteer guinea pigs! Good gracious! You don't know whether to laugh or cry!

Fia-Lotta Dahlman

One can only hope he is misquoted.

Casper Åhman

I don't think so.

Oliver Hagman

Attempts have been made before to develop a vaccine against coronavirus, without success. It hasn't succeeded this time either. The effect demonstrably diminishes after a few months, and then it's time for "refilling".

Nina Söderblom
Which gives the pharmaceutical companies the opportunity to earn tons of money for ever.

Oliver Hagman
It was probably planned from the beginning that the effect would subside. A vaccine that provides lifelong immunity, they make no money from in the long run.

Daniel Lundberg
2021 is the year when humans no longer have their own immune system but must rely on an unnatural immunity by getting vaccinated.

Vilma Andreasson
I quote: "According to Pfizer, preliminary data indicate that a third dose produces antibody levels that are between 5 and 10 times higher than after the second dose." Yes, of course, according to Pfizer, they indicate that! They are the ones who will sell the vaccine and make even more money from it. What happened to the "effective" vaccine that had an "effect for a long time" then?

Per Eriksson
Fighting a disease with over 99 % survival with a dubious vaccine isn't defensible. In Sweden, 60 % of the population was vaccinated against the swine flu. No other country vaccinated so many. In Poland no one was vaccinated, in Germany, France and Italy less than 10 %. Sweden had the same death rate, 0.31 people per 100,000, as Germany. In Poland, where no one was vaccinated, the figure ended up at 0.47.

Daniel Lundberg

Even though the overall mortality rate for covid-19 is low, there are still a large number of deaths because so many become infected. In addition, mortality is difficult to calculate. Other causes of death may be attributed to c-19, and how deaths are reported is also important.

Vilma Andreasson

Why do you want to manipulate an entire population to take a vaccine which we hardly know anything about? Why are such huge efforts made when you know nothing about the long-term effects? How sad won't it be for all vaccinated people to find out in a few years from now that they have probably become sterile or will die of cancer?

Pierre Dacke

Attempts to change the law are underway around the world right now to enable mandatory injections – even by force. The planning has been going on for a long time. Just before the swine flu in 2009, the WHO changed the definition of a pandemic, so that any virus can be classified as a pandemic, regardless of mortality. The pandemic classification in turn opened the possibility of using products that have only been approved for emergency use. And before the covid pandemic, the WHO also changed the definition of herd immunity to something that can only be achieved through vaccinations.

Daniel Lundberg

What the hell…

FRIDA

I will never forget how it happened. At first, I avoided thinking about it, but later I went through the course of events over and over again.

I and two colleagues went on a priority one alarm. All we knew was that there was a "lifeless woman" at a given address. On the way there we turned on the siren and blue light. In the car, we heard several patrols sign up on the open canal, but we were the closest.

We found the right house number and parked the patrol car outside on the street. Janne, who was sitting in the passenger seat, ran first, then me and Anders. Janne held the gate open, and I ran in. There I met a man who pointed to the basement stairs and said that was where she was lying. Anders stayed in the stairwell. Janne was just behind me, and I tried the door to the laundry room. It was unlocked. Janne was standing close behind me when I opened the door, and he announced our presence by shouting "police". There was no reaction, and we went in.

On the floor in front of the washing machines, a woman was lying on her back in a large pool of blood. I squatted next to her while Janne searched the room, which was empty with the exception of Janne, myself and the injured woman. Janne wore rubber gloves. He pulled up the woman's sweater and began doing cardiac compressions with both hands against her chest. In the middle of her chest, I saw several open wounds with traces of dark blood.

While waiting for the ambulance, we gave artificial respiration. I reached for the pocket mask and Janne placed it and started the insufflations. Suddenly I saw a movement outside the door and discovered a man in the basement corridor that ended about twenty meters away. He was armed with a large knife, and when I appeared, he raised the knife and came at me. *Establish contact, calm down, disarm,* passed through my head, but I realized that the possibility of reaching a verbal solution was non-existent. The man was pressed, desperate and perhaps loaded.

My pulse rushed. Instinctively, I drew my weapon and pointed it in the direction of the man at chest height. Bead and sight met as in a tunnel. The surroundings became blurred and the only thing that appeared reasonably sharp was the man's large body perhaps fifteen meters away. I heard myself shout "police, back off, drop the knife, lie down" several times.

The next moment, Anders was at my side. We ordered the man repeatedly to drop the knife, which he didn't obey. He moved restlessly from side to side and approached us. My gaze was steadily directed at him, at the same time as I saw obliquely in front of me when Anders drew his weapon, cocked the trigger, and took aim at the man. The metallic sound when the cartridge left the magazine and ended up in the barrel was clearly heard in the basement. Anders' hands squeezed the grip and his index finger rested on the trigger. He was ready to shoot and screamed. The space was too cramped, and the distance far too short, when the man, brandishing the knife, made a sudden, furious rush with his aim clearly set on me.

THE DIALOGUE

MATS: How were you during the time immediately after the event? How did you feel?

FRIDA: Empty. I felt empty. Sometimes I just sat, empty in my head like a shell. It would have been okay if I had felt pain or sorrow, but I felt nothing at all.

MATS: What did you do?

FRIDA: Almost nothing. I couldn't read, couldn't watch TV, couldn't go out for walks.

MATS: What did you think about what had happened?

FRIDA: I didn't think much about it. I knew I should, but I couldn't concentrate long enough to immerse myself in it and hold on to it. It just slipped away. But later, I have often gone through it in my mind.

MATS: What did you think about your situation then?

FRIDA: I hated that I had that indifferent feeling for everything. I had never felt that way before. I have always tried to find bright spots to focus on when life feels heavy and dark, but then I found none at all. Everything was just empty and grey.

MATS: Didn't you receive any crisis help?

FRIDA: Yes, but I wasn't receptive to it.

MATS: How did you feel about other people?

FRIDA: I felt odd and outside. I thought that everyone just walked on tiptoes around me or avoided me as if I had contracted a shameful disease. It felt like I was trapped behind a high wall, and I didn't know how to tear it down.

MATS: You became emotionally isolated because you had an experience that very few people have and can identify with.

FRIDA: Yes, that's how it was. But I wanted to be normal, as I had been before, and be treated as usual.

MATS: Mm. What did you think before the trial?

FRIDA: I didn't think much about it because every time the thought came up, I pushed it away again. I was expecting it to be difficult, but I didn't know how to prepare myself and make it easier. Everything had happened and couldn't be undone or changed for the better. No matter how long I live, it will remain. The only thing I could do then, and the only thing I can do now, is to try to accept it.

FRIDA

He asks and I answer. He asks questions that make me think back and remember. How did I feel after the incident in the basement? What was I thinking, what was I feeling? How did I experience the trial? I try to answer as briefly as possible so as not to bore him.

The only thing I still vividly remember from the trial is how provoked I was by the condescending attitude of the fucking prosecutor when he asked me his questions. How his ridiculous little show filled me with icy contempt, which, incidentally, turned out to be what kept me going until the whole trial was over. Instead of breaking me, he did me a favour. And I tried to pay him back in his own coin, so that he, through my tone and my way of responding, would understand that I was aware of what he was doing and didn't approve.

– If I have understood you correctly, Frida, your colleague Anders Nyman was ready to shoot?

– Yes, that's correctly understood.

– And yet it was you who shot?

– Yes, that's right.

– And what was the reason you fired your weapon at that very moment?

– That the perpetrator came rushing towards me with his knife raised.

– You judged that it was you, Frida, he was after?

– Yes, that's how I judged it, Thomas.

– And what did you base that judgement on?

– That he threw himself past Anders and stayed next to the wall

on the same side as I was standing.

– You had time to perceive that.

– Yes, I had time to perceive that.

– Was Anders Nyman's way of acting adequate, do you think, considering the situation?

– What acting?

– That he waited and didn't shoot when the perpetrator began to move towards you. Why, in your opinion, did he do that, Frida?

– I can't answer that, Thomas. You'll have to ask him, not me, about that.

– You haven't had any reflections on it? No special thoughts?

– The only thing I can think of is that he didn't have time to react when the perpetrator threw himself aside and past him, out of the line of fire.

– How had the perpetrator behaved shortly before that? Did he stand still or was he in motion or how was it?

– First, he moved from side to side and approached us. Then he stopped and stood still.

– And how long did you estimate that he stood still?

– Half a minute maybe. Then he suddenly threw himself aside and came rushing.

– Came rushing.

– Yes, past Anders, straight at me.

– Straight at you. And then you fired your weapon.

– Yes, then I fired my weapon.

– Okay, Frida. You are sure that's how it happened? There is nothing you want to explain more in detail or add?

– No, Thomas, there is nothing I want to explain more in detail or add.

THE NEWSPAPER ARTICLE

Police officer acquitted for lethal shot

The policewoman who shot a knife-wielding man who refused to give up was suspected and charged with manslaughter. The district court has now acquitted the policewoman as she had the right of self- defence, and it hasn't been proven that she did anything wrong. The man was armed with a 32-centimetre-long knife. The district court also doesn't question the fact that the policewoman experienced it as if she and her colleague were in an emergency. The district court further writes that "when she fired the shot, it was therefore both necessary and justifiable". It was judged that she therefore "didn't intentionally or through negligence in the exercise of authority set aside what applies to the task". All indications are that the two police officers did exactly what they were supposed to do. They repeatedly warned verbally, and when the man, who just before had stabbed a woman to death, kept moving towards them with a raised weapon, the policewoman fired a shot that hit the man at chest height, which led to his later death.

FACEBOOK

Marianne Åkerlund
Finally! Now I have received my second dose and can feel safe!

Mirja Mäki
Great!

Sally Persson
Welcome to the gang!

Eva Andersson
Super!

Nathalie Edvardsson
Same here!

Sally Persson
Thinking about how well you resist the virus after vaccination. Is it good to get a strong reaction? Does that give more resilience than not getting any reaction at all?

Marianne Åkerlund
A strong reaction is exactly what you want after a vaccination, especially after the second dose. It's a sign that your immune system has been triggered and creates immunity. The stronger the reaction, the stronger the defence.

Åsa Westerberg
Natural immunity provides better protection than vaccines. A large Israeli study shows that.

Kicki Hellström
Today my covid test showed positive, so now I have to isolate myself again. This is despite 2 doses of vaccine, social distancing, mouth protection and meticulous hand hygiene. I'm pissed to say the least!

Stina Roos
But you haven't become ill, have you? Even if you have become infected, 2 doses of vaccine protect 96 % against serious illness, and that's the main thing, right?

Malin Josefsson
On the contrary, having received two doses of untested emergency-approved vaccine (or "conditionally approved" as FHM calls it to make it sound a little better) carries a high risk of being stricken with serious illness. Thousands have already died from vaccine injuries.

Kalle Rosén
Now you have to stop spreading shit! Thought you were a sensible person. Deleting you as a FB friend.

Viktor Larsson
The very point of the vaccine is to prevent serious illness and death. That many would have died and been injured by the vaccine is just nonsense, misinformation, and conspiracy theories. If we don't trust science, research, and medical knowledge, we are in a bad way.

Ingrid Granlund
Great, Marianne!

Kevin Adolfsson
Now you can be close to people again.

Viktor Larsson
Nice!

Elisabeth Fors
Wonderful!

Annika Zanzi
You who haven't yet been vaccinated – just do it! Do it!

Karin Blomgren
Really!!!

Bodil Holmsten
Agree!

Annika Zanzi
Don't understand why you don't do it. Have never longed for a syringe before, but this time I did.

Bengt Andersson
Should be coercion.

Ida Fjällström
Those who get vaccinated do so for their own sake, to protect themselves Those who don't get vaccinated do so for their own sake as well, to protect themselves. We do what we do out of self-preservation and based on our personal convictions, not out of solidarity.

Lennart Lindh
There is no solidarity anymore. Selfishness and

self-interest are the only things that apply today. Then it becomes difficult to understand that the choices you make can have life-changing consequences for others. A "vaccine sceptic" I tried to reason with simply ran with the argument "I decide for myself over my body", an argument that is otherwise usually used in connection with rape and sexual abuse...

Bengt Andersson

Yes, vaccine opponents are dangerous. They must be fought. They believe that an individual has the right to break the law, just because he feels that way. The laws have been created in a democratic order by the government and all the inhabitants of the country must follow them!

Tobias Lutsar

What are you gagging about, old buffers? In what way would an unvaccinated person be dangerous to a vaccinated person? And in what way does anyone who doesn't want to be vaccinated break the Swedish law? In addition, it's clear as hell that you have the right to decide over your own body! It applies to ALL situations! Are you completely square, or what?

Ludvig Säfström

Everyone my age who I know has been vaccinated hasn't found out the facts about the vaccines but only blindly obeys what the authorities tell them to do. I have tried to warn them and pointed out that it's better to go through the disease and get a natural immunity, but they don't want to listen. They are tired of the restrictions. Those who take the vaccine say: "It's because I want to travel. I want to go on holiday. I want to go to the pub, to parties, to concerts, to festivals, to sporting events. I want a normal life." That's basically what people are saying. They don't care. "Well, there may be risks with the vaccine, but it may be worth it if we can stop this shit". Unfortunately, that's how many people think today.

Bodil Holmsten
Have you never thought about the consequences of the lies you spread? Opting out of vaccines for your own part plays less of a role in this context. Should you become ill, you have to blame yourself. But what do you think would happen if the vaccine program was suddenly discontinued? How do you think society would be able to take care of all those infected who would be the result of your anti-vax strategy? What should you say to everyone who becomes seriously ill because in your opinion it's better to "go through the disease" than to prevent it with a safe vaccine?

Siv Hedman
There are numerous studies that show that you are immune for a long time after having covid-19. Of course, they can't say yet that the protection lasts longer than the time that has passed, but many believe for a lifetime. Then why should those who have had covid-19 get vaccinated?

Annika Zanzi
If you don't take the shot, you risk the lives of others.

Karin Blomgren
If humanity ends up in a situation where it's a matter of stopping a life-threatening pandemic, and the only way is by everyone getting vaccinated, you must actually

think about your fellow human beings as well and about healthcare and society, which otherwise are getting into big trouble. In that situation, just thinking about yourself and not taking the vaccine is a very sick attitude!

Viktor Larsson
Vaccination is one of the foremost medical advances ever. People have forgotten what it was like once upon a time when you had to worry about polio, diphtheria, measles, smallpox and more. Smallpox no longer exists, and polio is largely eradicated. You should not listen to all the idiots in the anti-vax movement. They are morons!

Philip Gardner
"When the whole world is running towards a cliff, he who is running in the opposite direction appears to have lost his mind." (CS Lewis)

Bodil Holmsten
I have an antivaxxer as a Facebook friend. I haven't gotten into any discussion with him but instead reported his posts. Through that, he has been blocked on FB for a while, and what has also happened is that his posts are less visible in the flow, and he has received fewer likes. Trying to argue with such a person is a waste of time.

Karin Blomgren
Should we maybe ignore them instead and just let them get their covid? They can hardly make our healthcare system collapse now that so many are vaccinated.

Maria Moberg
Yes, why do you who get vaccinated have to attack us unvaccinated all the time? You are the winners, aren't

you? You should be completely satisfied, considering everything you are spared!

You won't be ridiculed, mocked, hated, offended, humiliated, belittled, excluded, displaced, get discriminated against.

You don't have to be considered selfish and disloyal and called foil hats, conspiracy theorists, flat-earthers, science deniers, climate deniers, murderers.

You won't be censored, deleted, blocked, subjected to hateful comments on social media, frozen out at work, excluded from the labour market, relocated, fired.

Still, you are not happy and have to devote yourselves to harassment and persecution. I actually wonder why...

Sofia Nordkvist

This is because when they notice that the effect of the vaccine is decreasing or even disappearing, they begin to suspect that they have been deceived and have to push all unvaccinated people even more to take the vaccine, so that EVERYONE will be equally deceived.

Tomas Bergman

It's easier to deceive a person than to convince him that he has been deceived.

Sofia Nordkvist

Yes, there must be many who begin to doubt their decision when facts show more and more (even if the media tries to hide it) that the natural immune system beats the vaccine enormously. Everyone knows that it's impossible to regret.

Bodil Holmsten

Those who don't get vaccinated and get sick and die

can't regret it either.

Karin Blomgren
There is nothing to regret! Everyone should accept this offer, both for their own sake and for the sake of others, and trust that our authorities know what's best!

Emma Nordin
You must be allowed to ask if it's true that there are no risks. If you don't get any convincing answers, and if the questions just become more and more, then it's not that strange that you question the offer. That you doubt doesn't mean that you are crazy or evil.

Sofia Wahlund
What's so frightening is the evilness, selfishness, condemnation and all the harsh words that come from people who have accepted the offer. Surely, it's incomprehensible and sad that those who have agreed to something that is meant to save humanity also are those (not all) who create division and discord among us?

Gun-Britt Andersson
I know people who took it only to be able to travel abroad...

Lisa Wall
An acquaintance of mine is now on a respirator despite (or because of?) 2 injections. She has been healthy all her life but wanted to travel, so she took the shots.

Johan Feldt
The Medical Products Agency:
"There is a much greater risk of contracting a serious

infectious disease than taking a vaccine. Many infectious diseases can cause long-term medical problems that persist long after recovery from the disease itself. Covid-19 has been shown to be a serious and unpredictable disease that has so far caused about 3 million deaths in the world, of which over 14,000 in Sweden.

The benefit of getting vaccinated far outweighs the risk of serious side effects.

It is better to be vaccinated against covid-19 than to rely solely on a strong immune system.

Of course, a good immune system can help us better resist various infections to which we are exposed. But it is impossible to know in advance if you have a strong immune system against a specific disease, and it is risky to take a chance.

Vaccination is the best and safest way to protect yourself against serious infectious diseases.

There are claims that the vaccines could alter your DNA. These statements are not true.

The mRNA-based vaccines against covid-19 (Comirnaty, Moderna) cause the cells to produce a surface protein similar to the SARS-CoV-2 virus, thus activating the immune system. There is no possibility for these proteins to form virus particles or new RNA. This means that it is not possible to become infected with the vaccine. When a real coronavirus then infects a vaccinated person, the immune system is prepared and can directly attack the virus.

Human cells cannot convert RNA to DNA, thus mRNA vaccines cannot alter the human genome. The mRNA contained in the vaccines is also broken down very quickly in the body.

There are no vaccines that contain microchips or any other surveillance technology, nor in any of the vaccines against covid-19."

Elisabeth Fors
I thought the same, Karin, but have been told that the unvaccinated are a breeding ground for mutations, and if they continue, the whole circus will continue almost as before. On the other hand, if everyone is vaccinated, there will be some sort of end to the misery. But then the borders must be kept closed as long as there are countries that have no vaccine. We won't get rid of the mutations as long as the virus has billions of unvaccinated people to live in. I think we just have to take new vaccines.

FRIDA

It became quiet around me. There was an emotional distance to everyone I knew. I tried to be forbearing and behave as usual, but I felt lonely and false when I hid myself and pretended that everything was as it used to be, although it wasn't. Some were troubled just by seeing or hearing me, as if I was a great inconvenience that you would rather avoid dealing with. It made me feel wrong and ugly. I knew it wasn't my fault, but it felt that way. As we all know, I don't talk about it! I wanted to shout. What are you so fucking afraid of?

I didn't know that I was so alone when it really mattered. When, for once, I needed help myself, there was no one to turn to. It was a shock to discover how great the emotional distance was to people I had thought I was quite close to. It was as if I had drifted away so far from everyone that it was no longer possible to make contact. It felt desolate. I tried to be patient, but sometimes I was filled with anger and irritation when I noticed how trapped with my feelings and experiences I was. Why the hell is there no one who can listen and understand? I thought. Why is everyone so fucking limited? I hadn't expected infinite understanding, but some openness I had thought would be there anyway. Instead, I was met by a benevolent but mute wall that I couldn't get through. It was as if everyone lived together in a completely different world from me, while I was alone and trapped in mine. Is this how a murderer feels when he has decided to keep to himself what he has done? I thought. Not being able to talk to others about the biggest and most important thing you carry makes you feel totally outside and isolated. But I hadn't decided to keep silent. It was those around me that forced me into doing it.

I could have sought professional help, but I didn't. During my two weeks at the psychiatric clinic, I lost all faith in the so-called care. The only help I got was to get out of the denial, and that help I didn't get from a doctor but from a young male nurse. There were no authorities to have confidence in and no experts to trust. I only had myself and had to manage as best I could.

Once I had realized how bad it was and had accepted it, I felt a great relief to no longer have any expectations of other people. There were no miscalculations and no disappointments. At the same time, I ended up outside all solidarity. At first, I tried to keep appearances up, but I couldn't hold on to that for so long. I fell silent and withdrew. No one got to know the feelings that stirred within me, and so it has continued to be. Mats is the first to whom I voluntarily tell it, and I do it only because he asks, and not because I think it will lead to a change.

In ten days, he will be free. What will that mean to us? Nothing, I guess. We will probably continue as before. I am waiting for him to tell me the whole truth, or if he doesn't know it, at least as much as he knows, because he hasn't done so yet. If he doesn't trust me one hundred percent, there will be no book. I have to make him understand that.

THE DIALOGUE

FRIDA: How do you feel now that you will soon be free?

MATS: Nervous. But I have had time to get used to it a little through the leaves and the overnight stays at Jeppe's and the meetings with you in different places.

FRIDA: Where are you going to live?

MATS: It will be with Jeppe to begin with.

FRIDA: Is he single?

MATS: Yes, currently.

FRIDA: Are you going to celebrate?

MATS: Yes, but only at home. Just Jeppe and me. I'm good at cooking, so I thought I would make an extra good dinner.

FRIDA: Okay.

MATS: Do you want to come and join us?

FRIDA: No, it doesn't feel quite right.

MATS: But you're welcome.

FRIDA: Thanks, but I don't think it's the right time for that right now.

MATS: No, okay. Maybe you and I can celebrate by ourselves on another day?

FRIDA: Mm.

...

MATS: Tell me a little about yourself.

FRIDA: You already know everything. My parents are dead, and I have a brother who is a criminal. I have worked as a police officer and shot a person to death, been charged and acquitted, and committed to a psychiatric clinic. I quit as a police officer, started working as an administrator at the Swedish Social Insurance Agency, and wrote a book about abuse of women. I have never been married, have no children, and no ongoing relationship. That's all.

MATS: Why were you committed to the psychiatric clinic?

FRIDA: I started behaving strangely and became a problem for my brother.

MATS: In what way?

FRIDA: I couldn't bear to listen to him and withdrew. I had done that before, for other reasons, but then I couldn't stand him at all. One night I just went out, and then it turned out the way it did.

MATS: That's when he lived with you?

FRIDA: Yes, some time after the trial, when I was on sick leave.

MATS: What symptoms did you have?

FRIDA: I felt blunt, as if I was living in a bubble. Some days I didn't recognize myself in the mirror, and life felt blurry and strange. And I had difficulty in concentrating. Sometimes it was completely empty in my head and sometimes it was so messy that I couldn't keep my mind in order and know what was what. And I had a strange perception of time. Past and present kind of flowed together and memories of events felt unreal and distant, as if it wasn't about me.

MATS: It seems like you suffered from depersonalization. It's a change in the experience of the self, so you temporarily lose the normal perception of reality. You have a feeling of functioning mechanically or as in a dream and not having control over your senses and actions.

FRIDA: Yes, that's about how it was.

MATS: We all have instinctive ways to protect ourselves from what's too painful to bear. A tragedy or loss usually takes time to sink in, so that we don't immediately suffer from full insight. The measure of anxiety required for a person to escape reality isn't the same for everyone. There is no way to measure how much shock is required, but there is a limit to how much each of us can take.

FRIDA: Mm.

MATS: When it comes to depersonalization, it's believed that some people have a special vulnerability to end up in that particular state under stress. It's quite common, but it can still be difficult to be taken seriously or interpreted correctly if you turn to healthcare. How did it go for you? Did you get a correct diagnosis and help?

FRIDA: No, no diagnosis, and no direct help. But it passed off anyway in the end.

MATS: Was it because of your reaction to the shooting drama that you quit as a police officer?

FRIDA: Yes, I couldn't bear to continue. I felt so lonely and isolated afterwards, as if no one understood and as if no one could trust me as a colleague again.

MATS: But wasn't it the case that you actually saved the life of your colleague or yourself through your action? Or at least saved both of you from being seriously injured?

FRIDA: Yes, it was. But then, when I got into that state you're talking about, I lost all self-confidence. Then I couldn't even trust myself anymore.

MATS: How did it feel to give up your job as a police officer?

FRIDA: Sad. It felt sad. And as a defeat. I had thought I was mentally strong and could handle almost any strain, but that wasn't the case, and I had difficulty accepting that. If I was so weak, it was just as good to quit, I thought. Then I wasn't suitable anymore. But I missed the job.

I put on my work clothes. The trousers with cargo pockets and the boots with steel caps. The protective vest with the steel plate over heart and lungs. The spiral cord that goes from the radio up over my back to the microphone, which is attached at the height of the collarbone, and the earpiece. On top of the protective vest, I put on a short-sleeved shirt with the police badge, and finally the equipment belt with the gloves, the handcuffs, the mobile phone, the keys, the torch, the pepper spray, the comm radio, the expandable baton, the spare magazine, and the service pistol. I pull back and hook the breech to check that the barrel is empty, drop the breech back, insert the magazine, secure and holster.

MATS: And now? Do you want to go back?

FRIDA: No, I don't think so.

MATS: Do you enjoy your new job then?

FRIDA: No, not particularly. That's why I try to do other and more creative things in my spare time.

MATS: Like writing books.

FRIDA: Yes. And to go back to that...

MATS: Yes, have you started writing yet?

FRIDA: No, not in a measured and structured way. I have made summaries of the interviews and such, but I haven't started writing seriously.

MATS: Do you feel ready to do it soon?

FRIDA: No, not really. How do you want the book to end?

MATS: What do you mean?

FRIDA: No one will be convinced that you're innocent based on what has come out so far.

MATS: Not you either?

FRIDA: No, not me either. You have been called calm, kind, honest, peaceful, sympathetic, helpful, ambitious, talented, nice… But that's not enough. I have met many pleasant men who have done extremely unpleasant things to their girl-friends, wives, and children.

MATS: Do you believe what Sandra accused me of?

FRIDA: No, I don't. But I think you know more than you have told me.

MATS: About what?

FRIDA: About how Sandra died. I think you know the truth. Don't you want the truth to be included in the book?

MATS: I don't know. The truth can't be proven, and what's the point of it in that case? Who would believe it?

FRIDA: Me.

MATS: I have had a very long time to figure out a credible story that could make me seem innocent. Why would you believe it?

FRIDA: If I feel like you aren't lying when you tell me, I will believe it.

MATS: You can tell by feeling if I'm lying or not?

FRIDA: Yes, I think so.

MATS: Using your experience as a police officer?

FRIDA: Yes, and by using my knowledge of you.

MATS: But there is no evidence, so that's not enough.

FRIDA: Was there no evidence when it happened either?

MATS: Well, maybe.

FRIDA: Why didn't you tell the truth then?

MATS: I'm not ready to do it now either.

FRIDA: Why not? It's you who decides whether it should be included in the book or not. Don't you want Maja to know the truth?

MATS: Yes. But I have difficulty deciding what will be best.

FRIDA: Then you can think about it. You can even decide that you don't want the book to be written, if that's how you feel. It's not too late.

MATS: Thanks, then I know what my options are. You will of course be paid in any case, for the time you have spent on the interviews and your conversations with me.

FRIDA: Okay.

FRIDA

Now he is released, but we continue to meet in public places as before. For me there is no difference, but for him it must be a big change to never have to go back to the institution again. I can't imagine what it would feel like to be locked up as long as he has been. I have tried to ask him sometimes how he experienced his time in prison, but he hasn't been very interested in talking about it, so I have let it go.

We could meet at my place now, but that feels like going a step too far. Or am I just afraid? We can call, and he has got an email address, so we actually don't need to meet at all. I can be happy as long as he wants to proceed. I will concentrate on working on the book and not think more about the idea of celebrating his release by inviting him to my place for dinner.

Viktor by the stove. Viktor at the dining table. Viktor at the sink. Viktor on the sofa. Viktor in bed. Viktor and me.

I like talking to him. Sometimes he lectures, but I have the same tendency myself, so I can't get hung up on that.

He has admitted that he hasn't told me everything he knows about Sandra's death. I didn't even have to push him. He knows the truth but chooses to keep it to himself. At least for now.

He hasn't said that he wants to back out, and I haven't put pressure on him to make up his mind and inform me. I may do it soon, but there is no rush. With my knowledge of him, I am almost certain that he can't refrain from giving Maja an opportunity to read about what happened. And for her sake, he won't be able to refrain from telling the truth either.

He must have known the murderer. There must have been circumstances that made him choose to protect that person. That he decided he wanted a book to be written may mean that the circumstances have changed so that he is free to tell now. But if he is like me, and he is, I understand that what he has borne alone for so long is hard for him to come out with. But in the long run, almost no one can refrain from answering respectful questions that are asked out of genuine interest, and I will use that, in the same way he used it last time we met when he managed to get more out of me than I was really ready for. That's how the male nurse at the psychiatric clinic did as well.

– How are you?
  – I don't know.
  – You know why you are here?
  – Yes.
  – You know what happened?
  – Yes.
  – And you know that it's irreversible and can't be undone?
  – Yes.

I have no defence anymore. I can't escape. The pain hits me with full force. It hurts so much that I whimper. He sits quietly and waiting, and I feel I can trust him. In his presence I dare to release my pain. When it is at its greatest, I know he won't interrupt by trying to comfort me. What I need are not comforting words but space to open and feel. I need him to show that my feelings don't frighten and overwhelm him. And he is there all the time. He is constantly attentive, present, and calm.

186

THE DIALOGUE

MATS: Have you been single for a long time?

FRIDA: Yes. Before Mum became ill, I lived with a guy for some years, but it ended.

MATS: Why did it end?

FRIDA: I don't really know. I had so much else... But we agreed to go our separate ways. Then Mum became ill and died, and my brother moved in with me. I was very busy then, both privately and at work, and was perhaps not really in balance when we happened to come across that guy in the basement. Maybe that's why I couldn't really deal with the consequences.

MATS: The consequences of your actions? The consequences of you shooting him?

FRIDA: Yes. I knew I hadn't really done anything wrong. I knew I had done the only thing possible in the situation at hand. But that I hit him so badly that he died, I had difficulty in getting over. That I hadn't done better than that. That I had to have another person's life on my conscience just because I wasn't skilled enough in my profession. But I didn't have that much of a bad conscience... Everyone thought I had feelings of guilt because I had killed him, but that wasn't the case, and I was ashamed of myself for not caring about him but only thinking of myself and on my own poor effort. Deep down, I thought he deserved to die, since he himself had killed a completely defenceless person shortly before. Deep down, I thought my killing was almost justifiable compared to his. I didn't know what I felt. I didn't even know what I *should* feel, and it confused me. I had nothing to stick to and disappeared into the darkness.

MATS: How do you see it now?

FRIDA: What I'm telling you now, I couldn't put into words at the time, because I was ashamed of my thoughts and feelings and thought I reacted abnormally. I didn't let it out, and maybe that was the problem. I was blocked by the chaos within me and escaped. Maybe I still do, although I see it more clearly now. Escape, I mean.

MATS: Why do you think so?

FRIDA: It's just a feeling I have. That I'm not really done with it. But I don't know. There may be other things as well, that I should deal with.

MATS: Like what?

FRIDA: No, I don't know. Let's leave it. It's not me we are to talk about now, but about you and the book. You have to decide if you want to cancel or carry on, and if so, how much of the truth you are ready to reveal.

THE GROUP

Emma Nordin
Is there anyone in this group who can explain the risks of the vaccine in a serious and scientific way?

Jonas Malmberg
I don't know how familiar you are with this, but the covid-19 virus has a spike protein on the surface that allows it to penetrate our bodies. If the body is then vaccinated with a small amount of spike protein, it forms an immune system against the spike protein so that we can't be infected by the virus. That's the idea. But scientists have discovered that the spike protein itself can cause damage. It enters the bloodstream and circulates in the body for several days after vaccination and accumulates in the spleen, the bone marrow, the liver, the adrenal glands, and the ovaries. Namely, the spike protein is a pathogenic protein – i.e. a poison – that can cause blood clots and bleeding and go through the brain barrier and induce stroke. You can also be taken with anaphylactic shock, which is a life-threatening allergic reaction, weakened immune system, pulmonary hypertension (which is a thickening of the blood vessels in the lungs that is 70 % fatal within three years even with treatment), life-threatening brain swelling, long-term inflammation and infertility.

Richard Ljung
Are you a doctor, or what? Anyhow, you have gotten hold of the wrong end of the stick. The spike protein that the vaccine indirectly produces isn't comparable to that produced by an active SARS-CoV-2 virus. The amount is millions of units

less, and there is no evidence whatsoever that it could cause damage in the way you describe it. It's misinformation and outright lies that you present.

Erik Källström

FHM: "Vaccination against covid-19 began in Sweden in January 2021 and there is great interest in the vaccines. Unfortunately, various misconceptions, rumours and outright misinformation are circulating about the vaccines, which creates an unnecessary risk of misunderstanding and anxiety among many people. There are claims that it would be better to get sick than to take the corona vaccine. These statements are not true. There are far greater risks of contracting a serious infectious disease than taking a vaccine. Many infectious diseases can cause long-term medical symptoms that remain long after recovering from the disease itself. There are also claims that it would be better to trust that you have a strong immune system than to be vaccinated against covid-19. These statements are not true. Vaccination is the best and safest way to protect yourself against serious infectious diseases. Getting an infectious disease involves greater risks than taking a vaccine. The benefit of getting vaccinated is far greater than the risk of serious side effects."

Britt-Marie Löfgren

I have had covid and recovered. I have heard that those who get it again get sicker than the first time, so I have been vaccinated. We who work in healthcare are under rather severe pressure to take the vaccine. Just like with the swine flu vaccine. But this is developed a little differently, so it still feels quite okay.

Per Eriksson

In just over six months, more than 70,000 possible side effects of corona vaccine have been reported in Sweden. On average, the Medical Products Agency receives about 8,000 reports of suspected side effects annually, and this figure applies to ALL medicines and vaccines. Never before in world history have so many suspected vaccine-related deaths been reported after a vaccine as now.

Some examples of side effects (several of which are fatal): Blood clots in the lungs, organ failure, heart failure, kidney failure, anaphylactic shock, myocarditis, myocardial infarction, lack of oxygen, drop in blood pressure, leaking blood vessels, partial facial paralysis, headache, blurred vision, swollen glands, hives, rose fever, spots on the skin, tremors in the hands or in the whole body, physical fatigue, urinary tract infections, weakened immune system, dizziness, flu symptoms, symptom combinations reminiscent of chronic fatigue syndrome, and ME.

Viola Löfqvist

I have a colleague who had heart failure and fluid in her lungs after her first AstraZeneca. She didn't really want to take the jab, but as a healthcare professional she felt compelled to go along with it.

Malena Lathi

I have become ill from the vaccine, which I didn't think would happen. I am vaccinated with two doses and have been admitted to hospital twice for 4 days each time the vaccine has attacked my immune system. My platelet count dropped both times from normal to extremely low. I have received 5 platelet transfusions and am now waiting for another treatment to see if it can keep the platelet count up. If not, I have to have my spleen removed. I am 42 years old and was healthy before the vaccination. Now I see the haematologist every week and get treatments.

Elena Kvick
A colleague became sicker from the vaccine than from the virus itself. Others became ill and had to stay home for a few days. One patient became ill and couldn't stay at home after the second injection. Another died from the second shot. Both tolerated the first but not the second.

Ragna Albrektsson
About a month after both injections, my sister had breathing difficulties. Had no one found her where she was lying and struggling for air, she would probably have died.

Doris Lindberg
Several in my circle of acquaintances have died after being vaccinated. One was only 62 years old and perfectly healthy before. He got a fever and high heart rate the same day he took the shot and a few days later he was found dead in his bed. The hidden statistics are probably huge.

Elin Robinson
People don't bother to report, perhaps because they don't know how to do it, or because they don't see the connection or because they don't want to admit that they have made a mistake.

Emma Nordin

I want so badly to warn and help, but even if my arguments are based on indisputable facts, I'm not reaching those concerned. I'm asking all of you who still haven't realized the truth: Read the statistics, read about the side effects, listen to all the doctors, scientists, lawyers, and jurists who say this is all wrong! But it is as if we live in two different worlds and speak different languages. No one wants to hear, and I cry and realize that I have to give up.

Ingegerd Mattsson

People seriously believe that one dies of covid-19 and don't understand that the vast majority of those who die are at the end of life and can die from any physical strain. I asked one of my colleagues why she took the vaccine and got the answer that she did it because everyone else does it and because she doesn't want to die of covid. But there is an equal, if not greater, risk of dying from the vaccine.

Elin Robinson

Yes, according to a study by FHM, the mortality rate of covid-19 is on average 0.66 %, if you include all age groups. Much higher if you are old and much lower if you are young. How much the mortality rate is due to the vaccine no one knows yet. In the long run, everyone vaccinated may become ill and die. And that's just as well because humanity will still perish sooner or later. If it doesn't happen due to the virus or the vaccine, it will happen due to the global warming. What has happened in some places in Canada and North America, where it was almost 50 degrees above zero and many died both from the heat and from all the fires that raged, is guaranteed to happen again, and not just there. And when it comes to the pandemic, it's still just as confusing. While some countries begin to ease the restrictions, others are tightening theirs because of the delta variant that is spreading more and more. No one knows how it will end. It's hard to live when you have two such big threats hanging over you all the time and you know it will only get worse and worse. But no one seems to care. It's probably most comfortable that way. People don't have the strength to admit that on the whole it's already too late.

Niklas Chopra
Exactly, Elin. The pandemic and the climate change are the two major global threats. After the summer's extreme heat, massive forest fires, torrential rains and floods around the world, an international group of scientists warns that the earth is already approaching "irreversible climate effects". Johan Rockström, professor of earth systems science, says: "The decade between 2020 and 2030 is crucial for humanity's future on earth." Does anyone seriously believe that we still have time to turn the boat?

Neil Davies
"Hey assholes. We've been telling you for decades that this was going to happen if we didn't reduce greenhouse gas emissions. You didn't listen and now it's all happening. We hope you're happy. Enjoy the heatwaves, intense rainfall, sea level rise, ocean acidification, and many other things, you fucking morons."

Niklas Chopra
And how is it that both the climate debate and the vaccine debate are so extremely "poisoned" and show two so diametrically opposed sides both among experts and among "ordinary" people?

FRIDA

Sometimes I allow the thought rest for a moment on the possibility that Mats and I will continue to meet when the book is finished. Not for the sake of the book, but for our own sake, just because we want to.

But I don't know how he feels about me. I don't know what he wants. I don't know what I feel and want myself, other than that it will be empty after him when we don't meet anymore.

I should let him help me before he disappears. He offers me help without saying it outright. The help would be that I opened up completely to him. I know he could handle it, and it's so clear that I am the one who doesn't dare.

As an adult, I have never taken up all the space together with another person. Well, once I did, and that was when the male nurse at the hospital helped me let go of the denial. He withdrew so that I got full space for my feelings and didn't have to consider his. That was what made me dare. And I think Mats would do the same if I showed that I want and need it. Actually, he has already done it. He isn't afraid of emotions. Not of mine, and not of his own.

But I don't let go of control. I dare not. I carry things that I may not have gone to the bottom of and should process further. Dad's disappearance, Sören's alcoholism and death, the separation from Viktor, Mum's illness and death, Fabian's criminality, all the misery I have seen and experienced as a police officer, my inability to trust and open up to other people... I don't know how much of it that still weighs me down and hinders me.

Viktor at the kitchen table. Viktor in the bathroom. Viktor on the sofa. Viktor in bed. The unused kitchen chair. The half-full bathroom cabinet. The empty sofa. The bed that hasn't been slept in. The emptiness. The silence. The loss. The guilt.

But I can't burden Mats with it. I can't. I'm the one supposed to help him and not he to help me. And when the book is finished, we may not meet again. I have to accept that. But I won't start writing until he has told me the truth. As long as he hasn't told me the most important thing, I feel some resistance to him, and that isn't a good starting point. It's no starting point at all for me, and I have to make him understand that. It's probably time to put some pressure on him now.

FRIDA

The first time in ICU, Carina was deeply sedated, but now the doctors, according to Moa, have removed the medications and are trying to get her to wake up by herself. Pain is stimulated at regular intervals and the reactions are observed, partly to try to get her to wake up, partly to assess the injuries based on her reactions. There is a risk that a part of her brain has been more or less permanently damaged since it lacked adequate blood flow for quite a long time. In emergency surgery, most of the blood that had accumulated under the skull bone was removed, but there is a certain amount left, and it must be drained away naturally, because as long as there is blood left, the bleeding can press against vital centres in the brain and deform it.

Maybe it's just as well she never wakes up again. Maybe it's just as well that she dies.

The man on the park bench can't be revived. He lies on his right side with his face turned towards the walkway. The face is bloody, and one eye is bunged up. He is wearing jeans and socks, but his upper body is bare. On the ground below the bench is a dirty plastic bag with empty beer cans in it, and next to it are Sören's worn out shoes.

THE DIALOGUE

FRIDA: How do you like living with your brother?

MATS: It's okay.

FRIDA: Do you get along well?

MATS: Yes, we do.

FRIDA: Do you trust him?

MATS: Yes, unconditionally.

FRIDA: Is he convinced that you are innocent?

MATS: Yes, that's what he says anyway.

FRIDA: Did the police try to find an alternative perpetrator at all? For example, were they looking for the guy Sandra told you she felt threatened by?

MATS: No, not that I know of.

FRIDA: Everyone thought it was you, even though you denied it?

MATS: Yes. Everything was signed, sealed, and delivered right from the start.

FRIDA: How did you react to that?

MATS: I felt powerless.

FRIDA: Your solicitor then? Didn't he believe you either?

MATS: No, I don't think so. He was stressed and rather uninterested, and I hadn't the strength to make any demands.

FRIDA: But being innocently sentenced to such a long imprisonment must have felt unbearable?

MATS: You believe I'm innocent?

FRIDA: Yes, I guess so.

MATS: But just believing isn't enough for you?

FRIDA: It has to be.

MATS: No, it doesn't. You have every right to doubt.

FRIDA: But Jesper doesn't? Doubt, I mean. Is that because you have told him the truth?

MATS: What do you mean?

FRIDA: Does he know who you are protecting?

MATS: That's the same kind of tricky question as "Have you stopped beating your wife?"

FRIDA: Yes. But I won't start writing seriously until you have told me everything you know, even if you decide that you don't want it in the book. I can't do it unless you trust me one hundred percent.

MATS: Okay, I see.

FRIDA: What would your brother tell me if I contacted him?

MATS: Nothing unless I gave him permission.

FRIDA: And you won't?

MATS: No, I think it's better to tell you myself.

FRIDA: Yes, I agree with that.

MATS: Yes, hope I'm doing the right thing now… There was a woman. Only Jeppe knows of her existence. He is the one who has kept me informed about her over the years.

FRIDA: There was a woman who had something to do with the murder?

MATS: Yes.

FRIDA: Has Jeppe had personal contact with her?

MATS: No, everything has happened from a distance without her knowledge.

FRIDA: And it's her you've been protecting?

MATS: Yes.

FRIDA: Tell me about her.

MATS: We met shortly after Sandra and I had separated. It was at a conference that we both attended. After that, we continued to meet. I wanted us to keep it a secret because of Sandra's jealousy, but Emma probably didn't quite understand how serious it was. I didn't tell her everything either, so as not to worry her. So, she...

FRIDA: How could you keep it a secret?

MATS: She lived in another town, and we always met at her place and never at mine. I thought we would lie low with our relationship until everything was settled between Sandra and me regarding custody of Maja and she might have calmed down a bit. I just didn't want to expose Emma to her malice.

FRIDA: No, I understand that.

MATS: And then Emma got pregnant, and then it felt even more important to protect her. But she didn't understand how serious it was.

FRIDA: Did you plan to have children?

MATS: No, we didn't plan it, but we both wanted it.

FRIDA: Was the child born?

MATS: Yes. But I have never seen him and never met him.

FRIDA: And Emma?

MATS: No, I forbade her to come and visit me. I insisted that all contact between us would cease.

FRIDA: And the police never found out about her?

MATS: No.

FRIDA: Was there no risk that her friends and acquaintances would react to your name in connection with the murder and contact the police?

MATS: No, I don't think my name was published. Almost nothing was written about it either. And I don't think she had told many people about me.

FRIDA: Jesper then? Did he know about your relationship?

MATS: No, he didn't. We didn't have much contact at the time, and I didn't want to involve him in the secrecy.

FRIDA: Who did you say she was then, when you asked him to keep an eye on her later?

MATS: I said she had been my patient, and that I was worried about her and wanted to know how she was doing. It was only external information he found out, and nothing that…

FRIDA: Didn't he think that what you asked him to do was strange?

MATS: I don't know. He is used to snooping, so it must have felt pretty natural for him, I guess. I don't know.

FRIDA: But Sandra didn't know anything about Emma?

MATS: No, not until that evening.

FRIDA: What happened?

MATS: Emma contacted her without my knowledge and told her about us and the baby.

FRIDA: Why did she do that?

MATS: I'm not sure, but I think she wanted to ask Sandra to stop harassing me and maybe she thought it would help if she told her that we were expecting a baby. She didn't know what Sandra was like because I hadn't told her much so as not to burden her. She noticed that I was suffering from what Sandra did to me, but I hadn't been very clear about what I knew she was capable of. I will never get over that guilt.

FRIDA: Do you think it was your fault that Emma contacted Sandra?

MATS: Yes, I should have told her exactly how it was and warned her instead of trying to protect her.

FRIDA: And Emma didn't tell you what she was going to do?

MATS: No, I had no idea. She had been visiting her sister, who lives here in town, and on the way home she went to the house where Sandra and Maja lived. I think she wanted to talk to Sandra to make her understand that it was her and me now, and that Sandra had to let me go. I think she wanted to help both of us by trying to bring Sandra to reason. Maybe she thought she would do better than *I* demonstrably had done. But I don't know. She didn't have time to explain it to me, and now it's too late.

FRIDA: But surely you will see her again now that you are free? You do want to meet her, don't you? And your son? If you haven't already done it?

MATS: No, it's too late. My son lives with his stepfather and his little brother and Emma is dead.

FRIDA: Is she dead?

MATS: Yes, she died in a car accident six months ago.

We get an alarm about a serious single accident. When we arrive at the scene, we see a burning car that has crashed into a tree. A seriously injured man lies outside the car, and a small child remains in the vehicle. The fire has spread from the engine compartment into the passenger compartment, and we see that it's ur-

gent. *The ambulance arrives and the paramedics take care of the man on the ground. It will later turn out that he is dead.*

The door to the back seat is open and thick smoke is pouring out. Both backrests are burning, and the flames are rising towards the ceiling. Henrik tries to unbuckle the girl's seat belt, but it's stuck and is so hot that it's impossible to touch. He grabs the girl, who is standing on her knees and screaming. Her clothes haven't yet caught fire, and Henrik quickly pries her free from the belt and lifts her out of the car and runs away with her out of the danger zone. She is red and sooty in her face, and she is coughing and crying, but she is breathing as she should and can stand on her feet. In the next moment, the wrecked car is engulfed in flames.

FRIDA

I am ashamed. When Mats told me that there was another woman in his life at the time of Sandra's death, and that this woman was also expecting his baby, my very first feeling was *disappointment*. She may have been waiting for him all these years, and now that he is free, he will resume his relationship with her and start living with her and their common child, I thought. I felt stupid for having imagined the possibility that *I* could have become a continued part of his life in freedom. I had difficulty hiding my reaction and don't know how much of it he noticed.

And then the relief when it turned out that she is dead... I am ashamed that I reacted so personally. What am I imaging?

But now I understand. It wasn't a heroic sacrifice on Mats' part that he took the blame for the murder. It was his feelings of guilt, and his love for Maja, Emma, and the unborn child that drove him. There was nothing else he could do. Considering how he is, I understand that.

And I know from my own experience what feelings of guilt can do. You want to be punished and freed. Both he and I have been punished, but whether we are freed, I don't know.

He is protective and loving and not a murderer. He will tell me what happened. He will want to include it in the book. We will agree. Now that Emma is dead, there is no one who can be harmed by the truth coming out. We give her another name and don't reveal in which town she lived or when and how she died, and no one will be able to figure out who she was or who her children are. Mats will be cleared in the eyes of all who believe his story. Maja will be able to read about her parents and draw her own conclusions. Mats will get his daughter back and Maja will get her dad back. Everything will work out. But I don't know how it will turn out for Mats and me.

– Here you are, Dad. I made this one for you.
    – Thank you, Frida. How nice you have drawn.
    – That's you and that's me and that's Mum.
    – Yes, all three of us are standing there.
    – I want you to come home again, Dad.

FACEBOOK

Joel Lagerwall
Now I have received my first dose of the Moderna vaccine! It's great that we young people can finally get vaccinated, you're really starting to see the light in the tunnel now!

Robin Hunter
Yippee, Joel! Here we come!

Ragnar Svensson
Yes, now it's only the vaccine refusers who need care and strain the intensive care completely unnecessarily.

Ove Jansson
Yes, think of all the hundreds of thousands of pensioners and old and fragile who more or less isolated themselves in their homes at the beginning of the pandemic and who still can't feel safe and secure despite having been vaccinated and despite making great efforts to not contribute to increased spread of infection. They are now forced to be surrounded by unvaccinated people wherever they move in society. There is no compulsion to get vaccinated, but those who without good medical reasons don't get vaccinated against a disease danger-ous to society should of course take the consequences of this and stay away from all social life so as not to risk the lives and health of their fellow human beings.

Matilda Wahlgren
The vaccinated spread the infection more than the unvaccinated because they move freely in the community now, while the unvaccinated who get sick

stay at home. And it isn't true that the elderly isolated themselves and made "great efforts" to prevent the spread of infection at the beginning of the pandemic. At Plantagen, where I work, the elderly flocked almost more than usual at that time and didn't care a bit about keeping their distance and other things. You couldn't help but think, when you saw an 80-year-old stumbling between the shelves: What are you doing here, old man, is it so necessary to come and buy flowers right now?

Sebastian Häll
Over 80 % of the covid patients in ICU are unvacci-nated! What about them shuffling off and taking their jabs instead of burdening the healthcare system completely unnecessarily?

Iris Ohlsson
Since all vaccines cause side effects, all vaccinated people also become a burden on the healthcare system...

Malte Bodin
Yes, 80 % of ICU patients are unvaccinated, the headlines say. And who are counted as unvaccinated? Well, every-one who has taken zero doses, everyone who has taken one dose and everyone who has taken two doses less than two weeks ago. In principle, EVERYONE who is in the ICU can therefore have taken the vaccine.

Alexandra Norberg
But oh my God how cheeky! You get the impression that only those who refuse to get vaccinated end up in ICU!

Anna Stenvall
You are considered unvaccinated 2–3 weeks after both

doses because you are as unprotected as an unvaccinated until then.

Malte Bodin
And all the vaccinated who have lost their lives during that period are counted as dead from covid or as unvaccinated in intensive care and are not counted as victims of side effects of the vaccine.

Mattias Laurin
Can you provide the source of your statement, Malte, that you are counted as unvaccinated until 14 days have passed after the last injection?

Anna Stenvall
And if 80 % in ICU are not vaccinated at all (or not fully vaccinated), then 20 % must have received two doses and achieved full protection effect and still ended up in ICU. Most people who are in ICU now have thus for a year and a half managed to not get sick, and then have the great misfortune to just after the vaccinations get infected by the virus and get so seriously ill that they end up in ICU. Is it so strange then if you suspect that it is the vaccine and not the virus that causes them to lie there?

Sten Sture
In Israel, 86 % of those treated for covid-19 are double vaccinated, their own official reporting shows.

Gudrun Hagström
And we still hear from the Medical Products Agency that the benefits of vaccination outweigh the risks – despite the fact that the authority has so far received over 70,000 reports of side effects (with over 200 deaths),

and despite the fact that the authority has only had time to investigate about a tenth of the cases. In 1976, 45 million Americans were vaccinated against the swine flu. At that time, 53 suspected deaths were reported, which led to the vaccinations immediately being stopped. The risks were considered too great. Why don't they make the same assessment now when the risks are obviously so much greater? The scary numbers are there, openly reported by the authorities, but no one reacts! It isn't discussed at all. Or is it me who has missed it?

Alexandra Norberg
It's scary to see how uninformed people are and how little responsibility they take for their own health. No one will apologize if you are taken with severe side effects later on and no one will apologize to you when you are about to die.

Ove Jansson
The fear of side effects of the vaccine is a virus in itself. A virus that we are defenceless against if we distrust the decision makers in society. Fortunately, most people have a natural protection against this, namely COMMON SENSE. Because of course we can trust the authorities, the healthcare, the medicines, and the vaccines.

Bea Thomsen
Reports in the EU's database of side effects show more injuries and deaths from covid vaccines than from all other vaccines in the world before this.

Sebastian Häll
In any case, many many more people have died from covid than from the vaccine. Just saying...

Louise Wahlberg

The worst thing is that children under the age of 18 can be vaccinated without the parents' written permission. Now it's the state and unknown healthcare staff and not us parents who are responsible for and decide what's best for our minor children. The "Offer of vaccination", that has been sent out from our daughter's school, states, among other things: "For students who are not of legal age, parent/guardians should fill in the consent form for vaccines. If the student doesn't have the consent of the parents/guardians, they can still get the vaccine based on the nurse talking to the student and assessing whether he or she is capable of making decisions about vaccination alone".

Bea Thomsen

This must be punishable!

Gudrun Hagström

No, unfortunately it's perfectly legal.

Jessica Johansson

Well, that's about time! My daughter and I will be there when the opportunity to book a vaccination opens up.

Eva-Britt Olofsson

On the form we have received from school, there is a box to tick next to "No, I don't want my child to be vaccinated." But at the bottom, above the lines where you are to sign, it says: "Through my signature, I agree to my child being vaccinated against covid-19 and certify the above completed health declaration." Do they think that we parents are completely devoid of intelligence?

Bea Thomsen
Oh my God, are there no bounds to this madness?

Egon From
Great that we can protect our children and young people by vaccinating them.

Hans Liljeholm
Super!

Felicia Malm
Very good. There are many teenagers who are just waiting to be vaccinated.

Alexandra Norberg
I feel so bad about this abuse on the part of the authorities! I'm so glad I don't have school-age children! How do we stop this?

Gunnel Rydin
Yes, it's absolutely insane! Our teenager would rather listen to his friends than to us parents. He can't resist the peer pressure. And he is not at all familiar with the matter and has no qualifications to choose for himself.

Ingela Törnvall
In my workplace (office), peer pressure is terrible. Once a colleague said (in the presence of the boss) that all unvaccinated should be shot. I dare not be open about not wanting to take the shots.

Louise Wahlberg
Oh my God! What did the boss say then?

Ingela Törnvall
Nada.

Louise Wahlberg
What a fucking milksop!

Ernst Isaksson
This is what the law says: If someone, your employer or someone else, asks if you have been vaccinated or asks something else about your health that you don't want to answer, you can say that there is confidentiality on that information in accordance with the Public Access to Information and Secrecy Act.

Gudrun Hagström
Yes, your healthcare choices are protected by law. Nor can anyone force you to get vaccinated according to the laws and regulations that exist in Sweden and the EU.

Jennifer Andersson
If someone asks if I am vaccinated, I say yes, because I am, both against polio, tetanus, and the usual childhood diseases. But not against covid-19 though...

Louise Wahlberg
Smart!

Sofia Wahlund
This anger and this hatred are incomprehensible. I don't understand what's the matter with people.

Jennifer Andersson
I think those who have taken the vaccine are unsure

whether they have done the right thing and therefore must constantly defend and justify their decision to themselves by attacking us unvaccinated.

Philip Gardner
"No one is more hated than he who speaks the truth." (Plato)

Ulla-Britt Johansson
One of my closest friends who thought I was selfish not wanting to take the vaccine said: "Hope you end up in ICU, so you'll see how fun it is!" We had been friends for 25 years, but we are no longer.

Stina Svärd
No, you can do better without such "friends"!

Camilla Eriksson
How do you deal with people close to you or friends on Facebook who harass unvaccinated and spread false information etc.? I can't bear to go in and argue with them that they are wrong. And if I were to unfriend everyone on my Facebook who shares/writes nonsense about the vaccine, I would soon stand friendless. Is it worth it?

Stina Svärd
I'm just ignoring them. Some that have made really rough attacks I have removed, but mostly I let them have their way without comment. I think they have read my post anyway and maybe learned something.

Marianne Larsson
Being friends with many who have different thoughts and

opinions is a great source, I think. If I only had like-minded friends, I would never get to experience something new and learn more.

Jeanette Fransson
One wonders why vaccinated people are so afraid of the unvaccinated. Have they not taken the vaccine to avoid becoming infected? Surely, it's us unvaccinated who should be afraid? I'm so dead tired of all the idiots.

Lizzie Lundmark
If someone tries to press me to take the vaccine, I say: If the shot protects you – why should I take it? And if the shot doesn't protect you – why should I take it? And if the shot doesn't protect against the spread of infection – why should I take it? End of discussion!

Jerry Selander
Clear as a bell!

Philip Gardner
"When you try to press something on someone, then something isn't right in the matter."

Jennifer Andersson
One hopes that something drastic will happen soon, so that no one can wink at the truth anymore and begin to respect us unvaccinated.

Ove Jansson
And for what reason do you think you deserve respect?

Camilla Ståhlberg
With what right do the authorities run this media drive

that EVERYONE must get vaccinated, and depicts all the unvaccinated as more or less irresponsible people who walk around and infect everyone else, including the vaccinated, despite studies and research all over the world showing the opposite?

Jeanette Fransson
Personally, I avoid hanging out with vaxxed people as I have menstrual pains and intermediate bleedings in direct connection with meeting friends and acquaintances who have taken the shot. This has happened to me almost ten times. Have never had these problems before, not even in my teens. Know several who have had the same experience.

Therese Schenkel
Except at work, I almost only hang out with sensible people. When I meet hybrids, I take pine needle extract. But it will be expensive in the long run.

Jeanette Fransson
Hybrids?

Therese Schenkel
Yes, they become half inhuman and completely stupid by the genetic manipulation.

Ove Jansson
It's downright disgusting to hear all you antivaxxers blurt out your dung!

Jerry Selander
Now we have been told by the "experts" that we are dealing with a virus that can only disappear if EVERYONE

takes "four to five doses of vaccine". This was stated on TV by the dentist and vaccine researcher Matti Sällberg, who is a partner in a company that produces vaccines.

Dennis Gordon
Seriously?

Jerry Selander
Yes, if you want to sell vaccines like blazes, you have to give people such "information".

Jennifer Andersson
Oh my God. And people just swallow everything. Don't they realize how sick it is? You think you are living in a tragicomic nightmare. How stupid can people get? Sometimes you lose all hope of humanity.

Jerry Selander
In Aftonbladet, there is a nutcase who writes that all who refuse to take the vaccine should pay for medical care themselves if they get sick with covid.

Jennifer Andersson
It's so idiotic that it drives you crazy! Then surely all smokers, junkies, alcoholics, overweight people, drug addicts, speeders, and so on, should also pay for themselves? They cost society much more than the covid sufferers do!

Mattias Svedjeholm
Everyone who seriously thinks that those who don't get vaccinated should pay for their own healthcare, I would like to ask to think about which society they really want to live in, because that opinion leads in extension to a

control society where all personal choices and actions are rewarded or punished.

Jennifer Andersson
It has become like a witch hunt on us. Public sentiment has been whipped up to the point that you are disloyal if you don't get vaccinated, and unvaccinated people are accused of being responsible for the pandemic continuing.

Camilla Ståhlberg
Yes, vaccine injured are classified as covid-19 victims and unvaccinated are singled out as super spreaders. Everything is to be blamed on those who refrain from the vaccine. A local moderate politician who speaks in the press says: " We see that among those who are infected among the elderly, it's very often unvaccinated staff in retirement homes who bring it with them to work and infect their patients." And when the reporter points out that you can be infected even if you are vaccinated, the politician says: "You can still be infected, but the risk is greater if you are unvaccinated. And we see that an infection comes into place and then the infection is passed on, that's how our search for infection works and therefore we can say that this is exactly the case." Great explanation, isn't it?

Jennifer Andersson
He must be misquoted, it's incomprehensible.

Jerry Selander
Yeah, but if you don't know what you are talking about, it probably has to be something like that.

Camilla Ståhlberg
Yes, what do politicians know about the virus? Nothing, apparently! But it's their DUTY to find out EVERYTHING about it, and not just blindly obey some selected authorities!

Jennifer Andersson
It's so stupid that it can drive you crazy! You can only infect others if you carry the virus! You are not infected just because you are unvaccinated! Both vaccinated and unvaccinated can become infected and pass the infection on! Is that so hard to grasp?

Camilla Ståhlberg
If an unvaccinated person is infected (and probably gets symptoms), he or she stays home from work. If a vaccinated person is infected (and may not get any symptoms) he or she goes to work. So, who is spreading the infection the most?

Kerstin Glans
One of the home care workers who came home to my 92-year-old mother was unvaxxed. It's on the verge of attempted murder, I think!

Ove Jansson
Agree!

Birgit Svensson
Yes, everyone who works in geriatric care must of course be vaccinated! Otherwise, they have nothing to do in healthcare. And wear a face mask and a visor!

Ove Jansson
Yes, all those who refuse, jeopardize the survival of mankind. Above all, those who work dedicatedly to save lives should think a little further than beyond their nose. But they apparently don't have that ability.

Jonas Malmberg
A study conducted at Oxford University shows that vaccinated healthcare workers carry 251 times more covid-19 virus in their nostrils than the unvaccinated, and therefore pose a greater risk to patients.

Gunilla Moberg
I end all discussions with vaccine opponents, not for lack of arguments, but because there are no conditions for constructive conversations, so to speak.

Jerry Selander
Yes, when the old arguments have been seen through and can no longer be used, that's probably the best you can do.

Peter Jones
"The biggest waste of time is arguing with the fool and fanatic who doesn't care about truth or reality, but only the victory of his beliefs and illusions. Never waste time on discussions that make no sense. There are people who, for all the evidence presented to them, don't have the ability to understand. Others are blinded by ego, hatred and resentment, and the only thing they want is to be right even if they are not."

FRIDA

How will it go for Carina? If she survives and wakes up, it isn't at all certain that she will be restored. It depends on how badly her brain has been damaged. A brain-damaged person can be assessed as awake after healing from the injuries, but she may have lost the ability to speak, the ability to swallow or other abilities, such as moving, walking, or hearing. She can also, despite healing of the brain, stay at a depth of consciousness that is judged as comatose as she doesn't regain control over, for example, breathing, doesn't respond when spoken to and only reacts with rejecting movements in case of pain.

I am waiting for Mats to decide. I should make up my own mind soon. I haven't decided on the vaccination yet, though it's already in full swing for people my age. I have tried to get as comprehensive information as possible, but all information, opinions, theories, and personal experiences are very contradictory and don't give unambiguous answers. It's virtually impossible to find factual and objective information unless you are prepared to immerse yourself into scientific studies and relevant statistics, and even then, you can't trust what you read.

At work, no one seems to be in doubt. Everyone is busy booking a time. The euphoria that some people experience after receiving a vaccination appointment or an injection, I don't understand at all, because this isn't about being lucky and winning the first prize in a lottery, precisely. Everyone has the right to receive the vaccine. But I am still not sure which option to choose.

When Mats has told me everything he knows about Sandra's death, and I have started writing seriously, he will con-secutively read through what I write to be able to comment, change, and approve. We have agreed on that, and it's high time that we start with it, I think.

What will it be like when the book is finished? What will it mean for Mats and me?

I am not very good at relationships. It didn't go well for Viktor and me, and it was partly because of me. I let my job and my involvement in Mum's worries with Sören take up too much space. I didn't prioritize our relationship, and maybe I should have done that. He didn't understand why I helped Mum to pick up the remainders of Sören every time he had hit the bottle and couldn't take care of himself. He didn't understand why it had to be me who picked him up in the drunk cell and drove him home to Mum. He thought it was her responsibility and not mine. And maybe he was right. But I was a police officer and used to taking care of drunks, so I had no choice, I thought, when Mum asked me for help.

I still don't know if I did right or wrong. Shouldn't Viktor have understood me and given me space instead of asking me to make demands on Mum that I knew she wasn't able to meet? Was it me who let him down, or he who let me down, or were we both equally guilty?

Sören is lying on the mattress on the floor, and you can tell from the smell that he has done it in his pants. The jailer gets angry and swears at him. He walks up to Sören and kicks him several times hard in the side. Sören moans and tries to protect himself with his hands. The jailer shouts for him to get up and disappear. Sören laboriously gets to his feet, and the jailer grabs him and pushes him out into the corridor where I stand waiting. "Here you have the fucking pile of shit," he says. "Make damn sure you get him out of here now."

FRIDA

Mats has given me a written account of what happened when Sandra died. I have his permission to reproduce it verbatim in the book if that's how I want it.

I don't know how I want it. I haven't decided yet. I understand why he has waited until now to reveal the truth, but I don't understand why he chose to do it in writing. Why didn't he just tell me, during one of our meetings? It makes me suspicious.

The report is detailed and credible. There is no evidence he could cite if he wants redress, but it isn't legal redress he is out for, he says, just that Maja should be given the opportunity to get to know the truth.

But there is nothing that proves that his story is true. By writing it down instead of sitting face to face with me while he was telling me, he deprived me of the opportunity to simultaneously observe and experience him emotionally. Was it a deliberate avoidance? Because he knows that I am good at judging whether a person is lying or not.

I don't know what Mats feels for me. Despite all the questions he has asked, and all the interest he has shown in me, I can't feel that we have connected very deeply. He is the doctor, and I am the patient, or I am the journalist, and he is the interviewee. No, it's not that bad, but the distance is there, and maybe it's my fault. I am not letting go of control. I know how it feels to open up in a conversation and trustfully start talking about anything that comes up and suddenly notice that the one who listens only does it out of duty or courtesy and isn't really interested, and how deceived and reprimanded you feel then. How sad and dejected you get. How you regret even trying. How utterly hopeless you realize it is.

If I show myself and take up space, I get a biff on the nose, is my experience. I mustn't forget that. I mustn't start hoping again and let myself be tricked into it again. I will know my place, which isn't in the light but in the dark. That's where I should stay and not bother other people with my trusting chatter. Getting an emotional blow from Mats, which I have opened up to quite a lot, would hurt extra, so I am not going to take that risk. I won't open up more than I have already done. I can answer all his questions, but I don't let go of my self-control.

THE ACCOUNT

Frida. This is what I partly guess, partly know, happened when Sandra died.

Emma had been visiting her sister and was on her way home. It was about ten o'clock in the evening. She parked her car on the street outside the house where Sandra and Maja lived and got inside using the port code she must have found in my cell phone. Accordingly, the visit was planned in advance and not just a sudden whim. She wanted to meet Sandra and try to bring her to reason and stop harassing me. We had talked about it, and she thought it might be possible to reason with Sandra. I knew it was impossible and asked her to stop thinking about it, and I was sure she had let it go.

I don't know what she said when Sandra opened the door for her and let her in. I also don't know how their conversation developed or how long it took before Sandra got angry, but when she found out that Emma was pregnant, she started threatening her with a knife. I don't know how it got there, but both were in the kitchen, so she probably just snatched it from the bench or got it out of a drawer. She aimed the knife at Emma and said that she would split open her stomach and "cut out the bastard". Emma got scared and grabbed the knife and held it up to Sandra in self-defence.

The next moment, Sandra fell to the floor. She was bleeding, and Emma panicked and dropped the knife and rushed to the landline and called me. She was panic-stricken but managed to explain where she was and what had happened. She said that Sandra was dead, and that she was the one who had killed her. I asked if Maja was in the flat, and she answered that she didn't know. I asked her to go and look, and when she came back to the phone, she said that Maja was sleeping in her bed. I knew she rarely woke up at night, but I didn't dare to trust her not to and asked Emma to stay where she was until I got there, and that she would stop Maja if she still woke up and tried to leave her room. I flung my jacket on and ran out to the car and drove away.

Outside Sandra's house, I saw Emma's car parked some distance down the street in a long line of other cars, and I thought it was good that it didn't stand alone but blended into the crowd.

When I entered the flat, Emma was sitting on the floor with her back against the door to Maja's room and was completely paralyzed. Sandra was lying on the kitchen floor and was bloody on one side of her upper body. I checked her breathing and pulse and found that she was dead. I asked Emma to go out into the hall and put on her coat and shoes that she had taken off and left there. I told her to go down and open the gate and make sure the street was empty before she went to her car and drove home. I made her promise to stay away and not contact me or the police whatever happened and whatever she was told. From the window I saw her come out of the gate and hurry to the car and drive away. Nobody else was visible on the street, and I hoped no one had seen her from inside the houses either.

I checked that Maja was still asleep. Then I sat down on a chair in the hall and tried to compose my thoughts.

The first thing I thought of was the phone. Emma had called me, which meant that her fingerprints were on the handset. There was no blood on it, but I fetched a cloth and wiped it a little carelessly so that her fingerprints would be blurred but so that the receiver wouldn't look excessively clean. When I called the police, my fingerprints would end up on top of her blurred ones. Then I thought: Can the police find out that a call has been made to me from Sandra's landline? I didn't know, but I decided to say that it was Sandra who had called me, and that she had asked me to come because she felt threatened by a man.

The second thing I thought of was the knife. I got up and went into the kitchen. The knife lay on the floor next to Sandra's body where Emma had dropped it. It was bloody, and I bent down and picked it up. Of course, Emma's fingerprints were on it as well, and I started cleaning it in the sink with hot water.

Then I heard Maja's voice behind me. "What are you doing Dad?" she said. "What did you do with the knife?" I didn't know how much she had seen, but I hurried to push her back into her room and explained to her that I had to call for help for Sandra and that she had to go to Aunt Birgitta and sleep there. "But what did you do with the knife, Dad," she said. "What did you do with the knife to Mum?" And I said it wasn't me who had hurt Sandra. "Yes, I saw it," she said. I understood that she had seen me standing bent over Sandra with the knife in my hand when I picked it up from the floor, and that she had misinterpreted it. "Mum was injured even before I came here," I said. "I'm not the one who hurt her." "But I heard you and Mum talking," she said. "There was no one else here." "You were asleep and maybe you dreamed that you heard Mum's voice," I said. But she didn't want to agree to that. "No, I didn't sleep! I heard you, and that's that!" I didn't contradict her but started collecting the things she would bring with her to the neighbour's wife, and so I went there with her.

When I got back to the flat, I called the police from the landline and made sure I left clear fingerprints on the receiver. I left the knife in the sink. I thought it would look like the killer had tried to clean it and left it there.

When I had called the police, I went downstairs and awaited their arrival at the gate. Have I thought of everything now? I thought. I haven't overlooked anything? That my fingerprints were everywhere in the flat wasn't strange since I had lived there, and other fingerprints, such as from Sandra's male friends and from Emma, wouldn't be identifiable. I might not have needed to clean the phone receiver and the knife, but it felt safest that way, and if she just stayed away as she had promised, I knew no one would be able to connect her to me or to Sandra's death.

I knew that Sandra used to let unknown men follow her home sometimes, so when the police came, I told them that she had called me and asked me to come because she felt threatened by a man she had met at the pub earlier. I explained that when I got there, the front door to the flat was ajar, and Sandra was lying dead on the floor in the kitchen. I also told them that Maja had been in the flat and that I had left her with a neighbour. I thought I was doing well, but the police officers seemed suspicious and asked, for example, why I had used the landline and not my mobile phone when I called. To that question, I answered that I had acted without thinking and that I didn't know why I had done so.

I was taken out of there at once. I was even handcuffed before being taken away. It was all the same to me. The only thing that worried me was that Emma wouldn't let me help her. I had instructed her as calmly and clearly as I could before she left and said that she had to give birth to the child in freedom and take care of it as if nothing had happened. I had explained to her that nothing else was more important to me than that, and that she had to agree for everyone's sake that I let myself be deprived of my liberty. But she was so shocked when I said it that I didn't know whether my words had reached her or not. I was afraid she would appear at any moment and admit that she was the one who had killed Sandra. It was in self-defence and an accident, but I still didn't want her to get involved.

And she didn't come. She had understood and accepted my solution and knew that it was true that this was how I wanted it. I loved her, and I have never regretted doing what I did. I hope she didn't have too strong feelings of guilt, and I hope she got on well with her husband and her children. When Jeppe told me that she was dead, I thought that both my children had lost their mother and that I, their father, hadn't been able to be there and give them comfort and help. That I haven't existed for my children is a great sadness for me. I have no right to meddle in the boy's life, but Maja I might get in touch with again. That's what I hope this will lead to. I want the whole truth to come out so that she understands how it was and that she was right when she said that she didn't dream that she heard voices that evening. But it wasn't Sandra but Emma she heard me talking to before she came out of her room and saw me standing there leaning over Sandra with the knife in my hand.

FRIDA

How do you know what's true and what's false? The fact that a person seems honest and convinced that he is right doesn't necessarily mean that it is that way. He can believe in a lie, which I have seen many examples of when I have read what people think they know about covid-19 and the vaccine. You may feel that a person is deliberately lying, but if his *conviction* is honest, you can easily let yourself be duped.

And how inclined aren't you to trust a person you *want* to be able to trust? I should contact Mats' brother and ask him to tell me about Emma. What if she didn't exist? What if the murder – or the accident – didn't happen at all in the way Mats has told me? What if he is lying to me after all?

It could also be that it was Emma who lied to *him*. "Emma got scared and grabbed the knife and held it up to Sandra in self-defence. The next moment, Sandra fell to the floor."

"Grabbed" the knife? How? To single-handedly disarm a person pointing a knife at you is practically impossible. How did she do it?

And then Sandra fell to the floor mortally wounded? How did it happen when the knife penetrated her body?

According to the medical examiner's report, she had "a stab wound on the left side of her chest with an estimated thirteen centimetres long puncture duct. Within the course of the canal, the pericardium, the heart, and the great carotid artery are damaged. As a result of the injuries, a heavy bleeding in the pericardium has occurred and in this way caused a rapid entry of death." Furthermore, "bleeding in the muscles of the back that may have occurred when the woman fell backwards and hit the floor" was detected.

Thirteen centimetres into the body isn't just a superficial little scratch. How could the knife accidentally penetrate so deep and hit exactly in the heart? That doesn't seem likely. A stab with force and precision doesn't indicate an accident; it indicates anger and intent to kill. I just can't imagine a scenario where Emma, when she tries to defend herself against Sandra's knife threat, manages to disarm her and that the knife then accidentally and with force happens to hit Sandra right in the heart.

I don't know what to believe. If Mats has told me the truth after all, he can't help me. Then he doesn't know more than I do. But if he lies, he is either lying about Emma's existence or about her statement. If he is lying about her existence, it was he himself who killed Sandra. If he is lying about her statement, it's in order to protect the memory of her. If it was Emma who lied to *him*, it wasn't by mistake she killed Sandra but in cold blood. It could also be that the murder was planned, and that both carried it out together.

Fuck, what a mess I have made of it! He must give me proof that she has existed. He must give his brother permission to tell me. I need to know!

No, what am I doing? I need no proof. What good would proof do? It doesn't matter how it happened. In a larger perspective, it doesn't matter at all. In a larger perspective, all people are guilty. We are limited, narrow-minded, self-absorbed, selfish, irresponsible, greedy, reckless, and cruel. Our good qualities have never been given the opportunity to take over and rule the world. We have chosen death and destruction, and we still do by the way we live. No one knows how it will end. Most likely, the disaster created by our blind selfishness can't be prevented.

THE DIALOGUE

FRIDA: Why did you wait so long to tell me about Emma?

MATS: I wanted you to form your own opinion without having received any explanations from me.

FRIDA: Yes.

MATS: Then I realized that a police officer rarely settles for less than a clear course of events and clear evidence. But in this case, there is no evidence.

FRIDA: No, there isn't.

MATS: And you're not satisfied.

FRIDA: I don't have to be. I'm just to write the book.

MATS: Yes, but I might have hoped that...

FRIDA: Why did you choose to write it down instead of just telling me? We're recording, aren't we?

MATS: I wanted to be sure to include everything, and that it came in the right order. I didn't want it to be messy and unstructured as it easily becomes when told verbally.

FRIDA: Mm.

MATS: I wanted to be able to read through it and change and

add if needed.

FRIDA: Yes, I understand.

MATS: Frida... What are you wondering about? You know it's just asking.

FRIDA: Didn't you have your mobile phone with you when you went to Sandra that night?

MATS: Yes, I had.

FRIDA: And the police took possession of it on the spot?

MATS: Yes.

FRIDA: And in it you had Emma's phone number?

MATS: No, I didn't.

FRIDA: But you did have telephone contact, didn't you? You called and sent text messages?

MATS: No, we communicated in another way. I didn't dare have any information about her in my phone, because Sandra sometimes took it and went through it. She demanded it, and I agreed to it so that we would be on so good terms as possible for Maja's sake.

FRIDA: How did you and Emma communicate then?

MATS: We wrote messages on Facebook. We weren't friends there, but we were still careful and deleted everything as quickly as possible.

FRIDA: How fortunate that you had arranged it that way.

MATS: What do you mean?

FRIDA: Because otherwise she would have been in your phone, and then the police might have checked her out.

MATS: Mm.

FRIDA: And it was lucky that she called you from Sandra's landline that evening.

MATS: Yes. Maybe she didn't even have her cell phone with her. I don't know.

FRIDA: Okay. And you lied to the police…

MATS: Yes, I did. I said that Sandra called me and asked for help, and I said that it was about a man she had met at the pub, and I said I thought he was outside her flat when she called, and I said that no one but me had been there, and I said that Maja must have dreamed that she saw me with the knife in my hand and that she heard me talking to Sandra, and I said that I had never touched the knife, and I said that I didn't know why I used the landline when I called, and I said that I didn't know who had killed Sandra – and it was all a lie. I tried to stick to the truth as best I could by answering the questions I was asked as briefly as possible, because more than ten lies I knew I wouldn't be able to keep in my head. Afterwards, I rehearsed them in my mind so as not to forget what I had said. Eight clearly stated lies that I had to memorize and stick to and be able to repeat each time it was necessary.

FRIDA: Did you make it then?

MATS: Yes, in the end I almost believed it myself.

FRIDA: Mm. You lied to the police, and you lied to me.

MATS: Did I? When did I lie to you?

FRIDA: When I had met Maja and told you what she had said. She said she had seen you with the knife in your hand, and you said that the knife was in the sink and that you never touched it.

MATS: Yes, I should have realized it wouldn't last… I picked it up from the floor and cleaned it in the sink to remove Emma's fingerprints, and I couldn't tell you that as long as I hadn't told you about Emma.

FRIDA: No, I understand that.

MATS: I told you the same thing as I told the police.

FRIDA: Mm.

MATS: Is there anything else you are wondering about?

FRIDA: Yes, why you took the blame for Sandra's death.

MATS: I have told you that.

FRIDA: Yes, but didn't you think of... One of the starting points in the evaluation of evidence in criminal cases is that it's the defendant's version of the course of events that is to be used as the basis for the court's trial, provided that the prosecutor can't prove that the story is incorrect. For the prosecution to be substantiated, it's also required that there must be no reasonable doubt that what happened has taken place as the prosecutor claims in the description of the crime and that there must be no other possible explanations. In other words, there must be no alternative course of events or alternative perpetrators. If you had told them about Emma, without revealing her name, and described the course of events, both of you might have made it.

MATS: No, I don't think so. Then the police would have found her.

FRIDA: But you were aware of the possibility?

MATS: No, I wasn't. Not at the time. And if I had been, I still wouldn't have tried to use it.

FRIDA: No?

MATS: I understand that what I did may seem strange, but I

couldn't imagine Emma ending up in prison. She wouldn't have made it. And I thought about the baby.

FRIDA: Didn't you think about Maja then, who lost both her parents because of you acting that way?

MATS: Yes, I thought about her all the time. I have thought about her every day and wondered if... According to Jeppe, she has been fine, but that both Sandra and I disappeared must have affected her deeply.

FRIDA: Has Jesper been in contact with her?

MATS: No, Siw didn't allow it. It's Maja's grandfather who has kept him informed of Maja's life, and it has happened without Siw's knowledge as far as I know. The reports have been sporadic and rather scanty, but I have at least gotten an idea of how she has been doing.

FRIDA: Mm. He seems to have acted as a real private detective, your brother.

MATS: Yes, you might say that. He has been my contact with the outside world.

FRIDA: How do you imagine the future?

MATS: I hope to meet Maja and get to know her as she is now, and I hope that I will get a job and find my own place to live. I want to wait to contact Maja until I have arranged everything. And until I feel ready for it, I think.

FRIDA: Okay. Do you want to continue working as a psychiatrist?

MATS: Yes, I do. I was struck off the medical register, but I will apply to be reinstated. And you? Do you intend to continue at the Social Insurance Agency?

FRIDA: No, I'm thinking of going back to the police.

MATS: I think you're right about that.

FRIDA: Yes, I have trained as a police officer, and it's as a police officer that I prefer to work. External or internal duty doesn't matter.

FRIDA

He lied to the police, and he has lied to me, and he has admitted it. But is that all? The story about Emma, that only I have been told, doesn't have to be true either. I re-read his account over and over again to find points of weakness, but it's so doubtlessly and clearly written that it isn't possible. He could have been polishing it up for a long time to make it so. I can't help but wonder how it would have been like if he had told me verbally instead. Would I have been able to tell then whether he was lying or not? Would I have escaped doubt now if he had done that instead?

He wanted the story to be as clear and structured as possible, and I can understand that. But if you tell the truth, you usually have no problem remembering a course of events. It's when you have fabricated a story that it becomes difficult, because it isn't possible to relive and remember an event that has never occurred. I haven't told him about the shooting in detail, but I could easily reproduce the course of events and answer questions that were asked in any order or disorder. I was there and experienced it, and I can recreate it in my memory at any time.

He notices that I am not convinced. He senses that I don't trust him. But he has explanations for everything. Some of them feel a bit far-fetched but may very well be true. I don't know what to believe. I have such difficulty in letting it go as long as I doubt him.

It wouldn't help if I talked to his brother, because he doesn't actually know who he was observing. Emma's name may be correct, but otherwise she could have been anyone. I only have Mats' word for that he had a relationship with her.

And why didn't he tell his brother, whom he trusts "unconditionally", that he had met her? I understand that he didn't want to do it after Sandra's death, but why did he keep quiet about it before that?

He didn't want to involve Jesper in the "secrecy". Yes, I can understand that. But I don't *know*, and I don't know how to be content with what I have.

It isn't for the sake of the book, but for his and my relationship that I want to be able to feel sure that he isn't deceiving me. He lied to his brother, so why wouldn't he lie to me? Asking for more details, such as Emma's last name, place of residence at the time, and exactly where and when she died, I can't bring myself to do. I don't need to know that for the sake of the book, and he understands that. I wouldn't need to know it for my own sake either, if only I were a little more trusting and a little less police. I am afraid that my distrust will ruin it for us.

What if it's true that it was a former patient he wanted to keep an eye on, and so he is using that circumstance now and letting the female patient play the part of his made-up Emma to hoodwink me. And if she is made up, he was the one who killed Sandra… That's why it's so important to me to have her existence confirmed.

No, I couldn't be absolutely sure even if it were proven to me. Even if she did exist, it isn't certain that she was the one who killed Sandra.

Why do I have such difficulty in believing his story?

Because there are too many convenient circumstances that allowed him to keep her away from it all.

Like no one knew about their relationship.

Like no mobile phones had been used the time before and

were not used immediately after Sandra's death either.

Like he managed to keep his head so cool in a chaotic situation that he could quickly figure out how to use those circumstances to protect her.

It's not fucking credible.

I am angry with him because he can't make me believe him. But that isn't his responsibility. I should be ashamed. I demand that he tell me the truth, and once he does, I think he is lying. What's wrong with me? Why do I have such difficulty in trusting him?

If I don't get to the bottom of it all, my lack of trust will become a barrier between us, and then we can't continue. If there are any conditions for that? But I don't want to be the one to make it impossible. Either I must get rid of my doubts once and for all, or I must find proof that his account is true.

The interrogations with Maja... Does his story correspond with what Maja says in the police interrogations? I haven't checked that.

THE INTERROGATION

ITR: Now let's see, Maja... You've been here and answered questions once before, but then we didn't quite finish, so that's why you and I are going to talk a little more today. Is that okay with you?

MB: Mm.

ITR: And what we are going to talk about is what happened at your house the night when your dad came home to mum and you. Do you remember that night?

MB: Mm.

ITR: What happened that night?

MB: Mum was killed.

ITR: Yes. What caused her to be killed then?

MB: A knife.

ITR: And how could the knife cause mum to be killed?

MB: It was sharp.

ITR: Yes, it was sharp, so your mum was injured by it. But how did it happen?

MB: Don't know.

ITR: Was someone holding the knife?

MB: Yes, Dad.

ITR: Dad held the knife. And what else did dad do with the knife?

MB: Took it to the sink.

ITR: Took it to the sink. But what did he do with the knife before he took it to the sink?

MB: Don't know.

ITR: You said before that dad stabbed mum with the knife?

MB: Mm.

ITR: Did you see when dad stabbed mum with the knife?

MB: No because she was already dead when he came to us.

ITR: Okay. If we take it from the beginning, Maja, you have said that you were asleep when dad came to your house?

MB: Yes, I did.

ITR: But then you woke up?

MB: Yes.

ITR: What woke you up?

MB: That Mum screamed.

ITR: You woke up to mum screaming. What was she screaming? Did you hear any words that mum called out?

MB: Yes.

ITR: What words did she call out?

MB: Swear words.

ITR: She called out swear words. And who did she call out the swear words to?

MB: Dad.

ITR: Did you hear what dad answered then?

MB: He didn't answer.

ITR: He didn't?

MB: No, cause he never does when Mum shouts.

ITR: How do you know that dad was there then?

MB: Cause I heard his voice.

ITR: You heard his voice.

MB: Yes, then when I woke up again.

ITR: Now I don't really understand? Did you wake up one more time?

MB: Yes, first I woke up, then I slept, then I woke up again.

ITR: Do you mean that you went back to sleep when mum wasn't screaming any longer?

MB: Yes, I did.

ITR: What happened when you woke up the second time then?

MB: Then I heard Dad talking to Mum.

ITR: Didn't mum scream anymore then?

MB: No, then she was sad.

ITR: How do you know she was sad?

MB: Cause she cried.

ITR: Did you hear any words when dad was talking to mum?

MB: No, I didn't, because the door to my room was closed.

ITR: You were lying in your bed hearing their voices but no words. Is that right?

MB: Mm.

ITR: Tell me what happened next.

MB: Then when it got quiet, I got up.

ITR: Why did you get up?

MB: Cause I wanted to meet Dad.

ITR: Did you lie in bed long before you got up?

MB: Pretty.

ITR: A pretty long time. Did you hear any other sounds then, before you got up?

MB: Yes, I heard that someone went out with the garbage bag.

ITR: How did you hear that?

MB: Just ordinary.

ITR: You heard the front door open and close?

MB: Mm.

ITR: Okay. What happened next?

MB: Then I got up.

ITR: What room did you go to?

MB: To the kitchen.

ITR: And what did you see in the kitchen?

MB: Dad with a knife. And Mum on the floor.

ITR: Where was dad standing in the kitchen?

MB: Next to Mum.

ITR: And he had a knife in his hand?

MB: Mm.

ITR: What did he do with the knife?

MB: Took it to the sink.

ITR: What did you do when you saw dad with the knife in his hand?

MB: I asked what he was doing.

ITR: And what did he answer?

MB: That he had to get help for Mum and that I should go to Aunt Birgitta's and sleep there.

ITR: Did he say anything else?

MB: Yes, that Mum was already lying on the floor when he came to our house. But I heard that Mum was angry and screaming, and then I heard them talking.

ITR: Mm. Now I want to check that I have got everything right. Listen carefully, Maja, and then tell me if what I say is right or wrong. Do you understand?

MB: Mm.

ITR: You were lying in your bed sleeping, and then you woke up to mum being angry and shouting at dad. Is that right or wrong?

MB: Right.

ITR: Then you fell asleep again and slept for a while, and when you woke up the second time you were laying in bed and heard that mum and dad were talking, and that mum was sad and crying. Is that right or wrong?

MB: Right. Dad said I had dreamed it, but I didn't.

ITR: No. And then, when it had gotten quiet out there, you waited a pretty long time before you went up and out into the kitchen. Is that right or wrong?

MB: Right.

ITR: And when you came out into the kitchen, you saw dad with a knife in his hand and mum lying on the floor. Is that right or wrong?

MB: Right. And then I had to go back to my room.

ITR: Mm.

MB: And then I had to go to Aunt Birgitta's and sleep there.

ITR: Mm. Do you have any questions you would like to ask me before we end?

MB: Nah.

ITR: There is nothing you wonder about?

MB: Nah.

ITR: Then this interview is over, and the time is 14.10. Now we are finished, Maja, and you can go out to grandma who is waiting here outside. You have been very good at telling me everything.

MB: I want to go to Dad. When is Dad coming?

ITR: If you ask your grandma, she can tell you about dad. Bye-bye, Maja, and thanks for your help!

  – *You're nasty! I want Daddy to come!*
    – *You know he doesn't live here anymore, Frida.*
    – *Then I want to live with him instead!*
    – *No, now it's decided that you will live here with mum, and then you can see dad sometimes when he has time.*
    – *No, I want him to live HERE!*

FRIDA

Yes, it corresponds.

When Maja woke up the first time and heard Sandra shouting and swearing, it was to Emma and not to Mats that she shouted. She didn't hear Mats' voice, since he hadn't gotten there yet.

When there was silence, Sandra was dead.

Maja fell asleep again while Emma waited outside her door until Mats got there.

When Maja woke up the second time, it was Mats' and Emma's voices she heard, and it was Emma and not Sandra who was sad and cried.

When Maja heard the front door open and close and she thought that "someone went out with the garbage bag", it was Emma who left the apartment.

It's the last detail that convinces me that Emma was actually there. Mats hasn't lied to me. I am so sorry that I have mistrusted him.

And I am ashamed. Deep down, I know he has been honest with me and told me the truth. My doubts have been there to protect me from full closeness to him. I understand that now. My doubts have been there to protect me from the frightening insight that I love him. I love him, and I love myself, and more than that I don't need to know.

Viktor then? Didn't I love Viktor? Yes, I did, but he *needed* me and didn't give me full freedom. I had to take it against his will, and that didn't feel good. I made him sad and disappointed, and that made me feel selfish and guilty.

Mats doesn't need me. He is free and independent. That's the difference between him and Viktor. And now that I have admitted to myself what I feel and what's right for me, I am also free.

Carola Gillberg
Got sick yesterday and feel lousy today. Should I test myself???

Bea Thomsen
Not with PCR anyway.

Fabian Becket
No, no, absolutely DO NOT test, they are full of poison. You risk getting seriously ill from it.

Carola Gillberg
Is it poison in a cotton bud?

Fabian Becket
Yes, they are contaminated with a lot of toxic chemicals. They have also developed a nasal vaccine so there is a risk of being vaccinated when tested.

Carola Gillberg
Sounds completely insane.

Linus Englund
Have covid with pneumonia. Fully vaccinated in May...
All the doctors said the vaccine saved my life. Been going through hell.

Mikaela Durling
I don't understand, did you get covid with pneumonia before or after being vaccinated?

Linus Englund
Like I said: All the doctors said that the vaccine saved my life.

Mikaela Durling
And you who are so young! This isn't the protection I expect from a vaccine.

Bea Thomsen
When the effects of the vaccine decrease, you can become infected, pass on the infection, become mildly or seriously ill and even die of covid despite having received two doses. This is why refill doses are needed to maintain protection.

Tobias Backlund
WRONG. It's almost impossible to pass the infection on. It happens but with a risk of one in a thousand.

Mimmi Gustafsson
The more people that are vaxed, the more breakthrough infections there will be. No vax is one hundred percent. It's clear that scientists know how it works. This has also been explained, as clearly as possible, so that we, who are not educated, will understand. Feel free to listen to the vaccine pod or Agnes Wold who explains in a simple way to us who are not scientists, virologists or doctors how it works.

Ragnhild Schneider
Thanks to the vaccine, I coped with covid-19 quite well, even though I was very unwell for a couple of days. I can't imagine what it would have been like without the shots. Don't want to know.

Beata Johansson

Have received two doses Moderna, became ill two weeks later, was home for three weeks, severe breathing problems, extreme fatigue, general malaise. Can't say that these were mild symptoms...

Vera Friberg

Got covid last Saturday despite two Pfizers just over a month ago. No side effects from the vaccine and it seems to be a mild covid with fever that has gone down but I still have no smell and taste. Am so glad I'm vaccinated!

Mårten Larsson

I'm concerned that the focus is on "I got covid but didn't end up in hospital and didn't die, thanks to the vaccine". Personally, I had the misfortune of contracting covid in March 2020. Since then I have lived with long-term covid, which for my part has meant physical fatigue, memory and concentration difficulties, brain fatigue, periods of fever, high resting heart rate and stomach problems. I'm starting to think I'll never get my old strength and energy back. Despite the good news that fewer people die after vaccination, the focus should have been on keeping the number of cases down. I fear that the devastating effects of long-term covid will only become apparent when it's already too late.

Ove Jansson

Regarding the ongoing discussions about the effectiveness of the vaccines, it's interesting to see that more and more studies clearly show that the vaccines reduce the risk of dying, becoming seriously ill or infecting others.

SVT: "The risk of dying of covid-19 is eleven times as great for those who haven't been vaccinated – compared to those who have taken the vaccine. This is shown by a new comprehensive study from the US Public Health Agency. Yesterday, the American Center of Disease Control CDC published three studies on the effectiveness of the covid vaccines. One of the studies has reviewed more than 600,000 cases of infection in the USA between April and July this year, that is during the period when the delta variant took over. The study shows that unvaccinated people run a 4.5 times higher risk of being infected with covid-19 than vaccinated people. They have also 10 times higher risk of being admitted to hospital and 11 times higher risk of dying."

Sebastian Häll
Yes, if only the foil hats would stop winking at reality some time!

Jonas Malmberg
Where in the text does it say that the vaccines reduce the risk of infecting others, Ove?

Camilla Ståhlberg
I don't believe it for a moment!

Ove Jansson
You believe that media, which are under the orders of press ethics, and scientists who would ruin their careers if they falsified results, are lying us straight to our faces?

Camilla Ståhlberg
No but I think it's biased and incompletely reported.

Ove Jansson
Well, it's up to you.

Josefin Ring
I find it strange that no one who is questioning this mass vaccination gets a place in the media or on TV.

Camilla Ståhlberg
Yes, isn't it? That's why it becomes so obvious that facts are withheld.

Jennifer Andersson
But surely people must begin to realize now that something is completely crazy? It can't be possible to deceive the great mass much longer, can it?

Folke Hjelm
Yes, I think it is. Even if people will die like flies with the syringes hanging in their arms, no one will admit that they have died from them.

Tomas Bergman
It's easier to deceive a person than to convince him that he has been deceived.

Tove Lindvall
Why must the authorities make EVERYONE get vaccinated? They must also have realized by now that the vaccine doesn't work satisfactorily and know that it gives a lot of horrible side effects? Why then invest additional resources in pushing it further? They seem completely desperate, and I understand absolutely NOTHING!

Tomas Bergman
It's a long way coming to admit that you have been fooled...

Camilla Ståhlberg
When they ease the restrictions (which is just window-dressing), they will soon start reporting new alarming figures on "rampant contagion" and point out the groups that haven't yet been vaccinated as the big culprit. All according to the agenda to get EVERYONE to take the jab.

Tomas Bergman
The strange thing is that all this is happening simultaneously all over the world. It isn't only the Swedish authorities who have been deceived.

Tove Lindvall
I don't understand how it will end! Or will it go on like this forever?

Jerry Selander
Yes, one wonders! But even if many continue to close their eyes to the last, it would be fucking odd if things didn't turn around soon.

Tove Lindvall
Yes, the truth must prevail!

Anders Holmberg
Fuck, I hope everyone responsible will be held accountable for all the shit when the bubble bursts!

Folke Hjelm

It's like a big IQ test. Just the fact that they are vaccinating already immune people and silencing all criticism should arouse misgivings. But no! Everyone will soon be queuing up for new shots.

Sebastian Häll

If all the blockheads just took their shots and then shut up, we would have no problem.

Vera Friberg

I don't think it's necessary to declare people stupid just because they don't want to be vaccinated. Some can't do it for medical reasons, others are afraid of side effects.

Sebastian Häll

Well, you have to declare them stupid, because it's in accordance with the truth that they are stupid. To refuse vaccination should be based on the fact that one has acquired deeper knowledge that provides support for a distancing. But when it comes to vaccine opponents, they do everything in their power to avoid even very superficial knowledge, and if you do that, you are both stupid and unintelligent. Call a spade a spade and don't try to hide the reality behind smoke screens. These people will never want to admit what reality looks like.

Folke Hjelm

Regardless of whether you are for or against the vaccines, shouldn't you still protect the democratic values? But Sweden's population seems to consist mostly of a bunch of nitwits who lack independence and who not only accept, but even praise, this development.

Tomas Bergman

"In a demokraturship, there are general elections, freedom of opinion formally prevails, but politicians and the mass media are dominated by an establishment that determines that only certain expressions of opinion shall be released. The consequence is that citizens live in a notion that they are conveyed an objective and comprehensive picture of reality. The suppression of opinion is well hidden, the free debate is stifled. " (Vilhelm Moberg)

Sebastian Häll

What the hell is a demokraturship?

Tomas Bergman

Demokraturship is a concept created by the French sociologist Gerard Mermet, and it denotes a society that is on the surface a democracy, but which in practice lacks a real and comprehensive freedom of expression. It's a society that lacks the opportunity for dissident groups to present their case on equal terms, a society that lacks a fully law-abiding judiciary, a society where you risk losing your job for the sake of your opinions and where you as a dissident or a dissident group risk being exposed to political violence by political opponents (and where the state turns a blind eye to this). Another characteristic of a demokraturship is when the existing laws are not complied with (by the state itself). So what we see now, is that the superficially democratic Sweden is in fact a demokraturship.

Folke Hjelm

And soon we will be a dictatorship. In fact, I no longer care whether people are injected or not. The only thing

I care about is the freedom to choose and the right to decide over my own body. If we can't agree that these fundamental human rights are important, then the fight for truth, freedom and justice is lost. Either you support freedom of choice and human rights, or you support dictatorship and slavery. The choice is yours and now is the time to make that choice.

FRIDA

I don't know if Mats is vaccinated or not. I don't know if he agreed to vaccination already from the beginning, to get his leaves, or if he had had the disease, so that he didn't have to take the first dose right then, or if he has done it later or has chosen to refrain. It doesn't matter to me, and I don't intend to ask him. I trust that he has done what feels right for him, and whatever it is, I respect it.

At work, no one talks about it anymore. As soon as everyone had received their injections, there was silence. No one has asked me if I am vaccinated. I guess everyone takes it for granted that I am.

Based on what people write on social media, I understand that different positions on the vaccination issue create contradictions in all possible contexts. Distancing, hostility, accusations, and discrimination arise. A couple of my university-trained and culturally active Facebook friends have turned out to be really limited and small-minded. It surprised me, even though I know that stupidity has not the least to do with class or education. One of them is also looking forward to start traveling again – going by air, that is – which further proves how dense she is. No one with normal sense flies anymore.

I have copied the most relevant posts from my two groups, cleared away likes, repetitions, and other irrelevant things and saved the rest in a file. From now on I won't refill it anymore. The content of videos, statistics, news articles and features in alternative media, I have to a reasonable extent assimilated but not included.

In some posts, I have improved the language a bit to make

it more comprehensible. If you have something important to say, but are careless with the language, your credibility decreases, and I think that's a shame. This strange time of uncertainty and confusion will hopefully soon be over, and therefore I intend to save my file so as not to forget what it was like. One day I might want to write a book about it. You never can tell.

What's going on now is going on everywhere in society, and nothing that I have seen so far has made me understand what mechanisms it is that govern the reactions and actions of people and authorities. Most of it is against all reason, and so it can't continue, I think. The truth must prevail in the end, mustn't it?

From what I have read and heard, I have at least come to the conclusion of what's right for me to do regarding the vaccination. I have been open to information from all sides and have felt which assertions my inner self has rebelled against, and which have resonated within me, and that has settled the matter. I don't need to find out more. Now I will concentrate on working on the book and trying to finish it. It has been hard, while writing, to follow my two groups online and select the most important information and take it in, so it's a relief that I don't have to do that anymore.

In a larger perspective, it doesn't matter at all how I feel or what I get engaged in. In a larger perspective, a single person doesn't matter at all. The future is as uncertain as it has always been, although we are now beginning to predict how it will end. Man's time on earth is probably soon over, and I don't think there is much we can do to prevent it.